GOING BACKWARDS

GOING BACKWARDS

Jacki Kelly
Copyright 2015 by Kelly, Jacki
ISBN: 978-1-942202-05-9
First Edition Electronic August 2015
Published by Yobachi Publishing, LLC

Other Books By Jacki Kelly

THE SWEET ROAD SERIES
The Sweet Road Home
The Sweet Road To Love
The Sweet Road Back

DATING JUST GOT SERIOUS
Blind Date
One Date At A Time
Date Me
A Single Date
Speed Date
Dating Just Got Serious – Box Set

WOMEN'S FICTION
Packed and Ready To Go

For Gregg, for all the forever's

Trust dies but mistrust blossoms.

Sophocles

Chapter One - Crystal

I was turning into my mother. For some people that would have been a happy thought. I would rather tear open my chest and pull my heart out with my bare hands than let someone walk all over it and tell me they love me at the same time.

It was a reality I could have done without.

I ran my hand down Max's chest. We had just enough time for a quickie before he left for work. I caressed his morning woody, massaging it slowly enough to arouse him.

"Crystal, I can't this morning. I have to go in early. If I don't finish the deposition on the Royal case, I can't tell the firm it was because my wife wouldn't let me out of bed." He placed his hand over mine and pulled it away before climbing over me and heading toward the bathroom. "It would be nice if my wife could have breakfast ready before I leave the apartment." He was everything I wanted in a man, tall, handsome enough to turn heads, dark hair and eyes that accentuated his chocolate complexion, but lately I didn't seem to be enough for him. Maybe he no longer found my skinny legs or narrow hips attractive.

Max's rejection was so nice I didn't want to cry this time. Marrying the most polite man on the east coast had its benefits. It softened the blow when I slipped from being the star in his life to being the woman he dragged home to late at night, when he was too tired to see I'd waxed every part of my body just for him, stayed up late with heavy eyelids just for him, would do anything, even look foolish, just for him.

This wasn't the life I thought I would be living at twenty-two. The two of us should be still combing the bars into the wee morning hours and heading off to work too hung-over to care about mortgages and or savings funds.

Swinging my legs over the side of the bed, I asked, "What time will you be home tonight?"

"Don't wait up for me. It might be late," he yelled through the door.

"That's the same thing you said last night, and the night before, and the night before that."

"You knew there would be days like this. I warned you." His response sounded like my concerns were the least of his worries.

When had our marriage become such a burden for him? The fun, carefree Max disappeared for weeks at a time, leaving behind a conservative stranger I hardly recognized. He was so obsessed with saving money and making partner and getting a larger apartment that he seemed to forget the promises we'd made on the warm sands during our honeymoon. We weren't going to become our parents and we were always going to put each other first. But now that sounded like a different couple in a different place at a different time.

I was growing impatient with all the waiting. If my mother had been a little less patient and a lot more diligent, she could have saved herself a lot of heartache. I had no intention of being just like my mother.

Walking from the bedroom to the kitchen took seconds, but it was long enough to remember all the good stuff. The good stuff that had walked with us down the church aisle, went to Hawaii on our honeymoon, moved into the tiny two bedroom apartment on New York's east side with us. But all the good stuff was gone, used up by neglect.

The kitchen, like every other room in the apartment with a window, looked out on the brick wall of the building next door. I cracked the window to allow the smell of fresh bread from the bakery to tickle my nose. It seemed like such a small thing, but it always made me smile.

From the cabinet over the refrigerator I removed a box of Cheerios and set it on the table next to the quart of skim milk. I was almost out of the kitchen when I remembered the bowl and spoon. I returned and placed them on the table next to the cereal.

In the bedroom, I pulled on my sweats and running shoes. I was tying my hair in a bun when Max called me from the kitchen.

He had his back to me when I walked in. "Yeah,

babe?"

"Is this your idea of breakfast?" He spun around and shoved a spoonful of cereal into his mouth.

"You said you were in a hurry." I shrugged a shoulder. My tone should have let him know we were having a silent tug of war, again.

He put the empty bowl into the sink, then pulled me close, wrapping his arms around my waist.

"I'll make dinner reservations at your favorite restaurant, BoBo. Let's meet there at seven tonight. Will that put a smile on your face?"

"Yes, yes." My voice was squeaky with delight. "But I thought you had to work late. You just said—"

"My beautiful wife comes first." He looked down in my eyes and pushed my hair off my forehead. And just like that I forgave him. I draped my arms around his neck and he kissed my lips, then slipped his tongue in my mouth. The sweet taste of milk lingered on his tongue.

I drew back and looked up at him. "We haven't been out in a long time. I'm so excited."

"Crystal, we went to the Chelsea Market last week. You even bought brownies. Remember?"

"If we buy groceries for the house, it doesn't count. Tonight, I get to dress up."

He made the face that said he thought I was being bratty before kissing my forehead.

"Oh, okay. Don't be late." He pulled on his suit jacket, picked up his briefcase, and was out the door before I could think of a witty retort.

I'm never late. We missed the movie last week because by the time he got home, the show had already started.

I laced up my sneakers, then shoved the apartment key and my ID into my pocket. With my phone in my hand, I was out the door.

I hit my favorite path in Central Park and all the fussing from this morning disappeared. All I needed was a job to fill my empty days. It shouldn't have taken so long to find something. I had experience, a degree, impeccable references, and nobody was perkier than me.

I rounded the path and almost ran into Dexter. Several times a week we jogged together if our paths crossed. Someone at Max's firm had recommended him to paint our condo when we moved in. He introduced me to colors I would never have thought about for the kitchen and the bedroom. The warmest shades of gray and pink gave the bedroom a romantic aura even though there was very little romance going on in it.

Dexter was the boyfriend in my head. With his olive complexion and shoulder-length blond hair, I couldn't explain the attraction, but I couldn't ignore it either. He was a backup man just in case I grew bored, or just in case Max slipped into an endless coma, or even worse, just in case Max dropped dead. As long as he stayed in my fantasies it was acceptable and I didn't need to do any Hail Mary's.

"Hello gorgeous. Are you trying to increase your pace? You almost blew right past me?" Dexter had the sexiest grin outside of Max. But Dexter was carefree and always available. There were a few drawbacks with the little fantasy I often unleashed in my head. I was married, I loved Max, and even though Dexter was tall and Hollywood handsome, his ambition was on par with a dog with a limp. He was only interested if it was placed right at the tip of his nose. How he kept his small house painting business afloat was a mystery. He never seemed to work.

At the end of three miles my clothes were soaked, my hair was plastered against my head, and I was drained. I plopped into the first available bench and bent over to catch my breath.

"Calling it quits already?" Dexter jogged around me. He didn't even sound winded. He stopped, bent at the waist to look in my face. His lips were just inches from mine. I could have pretended to fall right into their lushness. "What is it? What's bothering you?"

I rested my hands on my knees. "Everything and nothing. How's that for an answer?"

"Tell me more."

"Living in New York was supposed to be glamorous. Nothing has turned out the way I imagined. And Max doesn't seem to care and he's never home."

Dexter grabbed me by the hand and tugged me

toward the little cafe where we often shared bear claws after our run.

When we were seated, he poured two packs of raw brown sugar into his black coffee without taking his eyes off me. "How long are we going to sit here before you let loose?"

"I gave you the whole story. I'm supposed to be happy and I'm not. We haven't been married long enough for it to be falling apart already."

"Are you upset you don't have a job, or has Max done something?" He leaned back in his chair as if my reply required lots of space.

I picked up several artificial sugar packets and stacked them on top of each other. "I've told you about my parents and the ugly mess they made of their lives. I've only just started talking to my dad again and that's only because of my little sister, Kia." I shook my head. "Anyway, I feel like we're becoming like my parents."

"You think Max is cheating on you?" Dexter sounded more interested now.

His words hit me in the gut. "I don't know what I think. I…I…he wouldn't, not after what my father put us through."

Dexter shrugged his shoulders. He wasn't buying my reasoning, but he wouldn't tell me so. "Always verify, Crystal. Always." He picked up his cup, drained it, then leaned back in his chair and dropped the cup in the trash. "If you need a job, I could use some help."

"Yeah, right. I can't paint the back side of a barn."

"I wasn't talking about painting. I need an assistant. Someone to keep track of the appointments, the colors, the payments. It pays better than minimum wage." He rested his elbows on the table and locked eyes with me. I knew I should say no. Dexter's intentions weren't purely altruistic and I should know. The way he always let his hand linger on my back wasn't for moral support.

"Look, I've got to run. Think about it and give me a call. You've got my number." He kissed me on the mouth and disappeared out the door.

####

The last time I'd dressed up for Max was for one of his firm's dinner parties. I remember feeling very prim and proper all night. He was adamant that I not reveal too much, so I was buttoned up and zipped up so tight I could hardly breathe. Tonight, I didn't have to look like a recovering nun, so I slipped on the sexiest dress in my tiny closet. The deep V-cut exposed my breasts. My best assets. The emerald green color made me sparkle, and tonight I wanted to remind Max of all the things he said he loved about me.

The dress was much too revealing for the subway,

so I splurged and hailed a cab on the corner. The excitement in my stomach reminded me of our first date. Max had been just as excited. He'd stumbled over his words all night. But his persistence won me over. Somewhere behind all the cases, the briefs, the court appearances, and the long hours, that same person still existed. I saw it in the fleeting moments when he relaxed.

In the West Village, traffic slowed and grew thick as we neared Sheridan Square. I tapped on the plastic shield and asked to be let out. Even in my four-inch heels I could walk the two blocks to BoBo's. I paid the fare and hopped out.

The small restaurant located in what used to be a townhouse was known for its fine French food. True to his word, Max had made the reservation and even though I was twenty minutes late, he wasn't there yet. Not surprising. Something always held him up. It used to be me, now it was his career.

I was escorted upstairs to a small table jammed into a corner. Every time we came, we were seated at the same table. I wondered if Max had requested it for our romantic evening.

I ordered two Manhattans and waited.

Dexter's job offer wasn't something to get excited about, but it would give me something to fill my days until my career took off. I was beginning to wonder if that was ever going to happen. The publishing industry was in such turmoil maybe I needed to reconsider my choices. But working with Dexter was just as crazy. What would Max think of the idea? He didn't really know Dexter. He was too busy at work to care what color I painted the condo. But I'd given him enough stories about Dexter's antics although he always half-listened and nodded his head until I grew silent.

Over the roar of conversation in the congested space, I picked up the chime of my phone. I hesitated before opening my clutch.

Max was an hour late.

"Where are you?" I whispered into the phone.

"Don't get mad, Crystal, but I'm still at the office. I don't think I'm going to make it. I've been trying to call you for twenty minutes."

"I have the ringer down low, so I couldn't hear it. Do you mean you're not coming at all?" I didn't want to sound like a whiny child, but my disappointment edged out my ability to restrain it.

"Go ahead and have dinner. Since you're there it makes sense. Order the same thing for me, but get it to go. I'll eat when I get home. I'm sorry, Crystal. I'll make it up to you." The phones ringing in the background validated he was in the office the constant ringing always drove me crazy.

I nodded and pushed back tears.

"Crystal, did you hear me?" He sounded rushed.

"Yes. I heard you." I ended the call without a good-bye. I paid for the drinks and walked out.

It took me almost a half an hour to catch a cab. The night was cool and my attempt to look sexy only looked crazy as I pulled my flimsy scarf tight around my shoulders.

"Where to?" the cab driver asked over his shoulder.

"West 78th Street…no change that. Please take me to the corner of Wall Street and Water Street. And please hurry." The skin at the base of my back itched. I'd promised I wouldn't do this anymore, but every instinct in my body demanded I do it. I had no desire to cause a scene, or yell at the top of my lungs, or scratch or kick. I only wanted to know if Max was bent over his desk, cluttered in papers, and stacked with his expensive law books.

Once I witnessed that with my own eyes, I could go home, go to bed and not become a raging lunatic obsessing about what I thought was going on. My mother would have gone home and waited—a glass of wine at her fingertips and a box of tissues on her bedside table.

The more I thought about what my mother wouldn't do, the more I knew I was doing the right thing.

Since it was after nine, traffic wasn't nearly as thick. The closer we got, the faster my heart raced. By the time the driver slowed and turned onto Water Street, I was gasping. If Max was behind his desk working, he'd be so angry at me, he'd probably want

11

a divorce—that's what he threatened the last time I showed up unannounced. If he wasn't there, this might just be the push I needed to walk away.

I paid the driver. "Can you wait for me?"

"How long are you going to be?"

I gave him an extra twenty. "If I'm not back by the time this is used up, you can leave."

He nodded and I hopped out. The small parking lot out front was empty. There weren't even any cars from the service waiting to take the late night lawyers home. Didn't he know I'd check? How long did he think he could fool me? Twenty years?

"Good evening, ma'am, who are you hear to see this time of night?"

"I'm going up to Walchoff and Finestein, to see my husband." I scribbled my name on the log without looking at the guard.

"The offices are all closed. There's no one up there. We just did a sweep of those floors and shut down the Teleprompters."

"Are you sure? My husband said he was working late." I looked around the lobby. Usually this building was teaming with people, tonight it was strangely quiet, locked down, buttoned up like a vault.

"Yeah. I'm sure." His gruff tone left no room to contest him. It was enough to make me drop the pen and hurry back to the cab.

Chapter Two - Walter

The highlight of my weekend used to be getting up early and heading to the Country Club before the honey-do list could make waste of my plans. Those were the good old days. If I had half as much money as I used to have, I'd buy those days back again.

This morning Sasha was on her side of the bed, her knees clamped together tight, making sure I didn't get any ideas and think she was willing to have some morning sex. If my wake-up boner saw any satisfaction it would happen in the shower, like yesterday.

"Are you going to get the baby? It's your turn and she's been crying for almost a minute." Sasha kicked my ankle and flipped over, taking the cover sheet with her.

"She's a year old, why can't she sleep later?"

"You can ask her when you go in there."

Payback was a bitch and I'd been bitch slapped. The good life was better when I only enjoyed it in small doses. Up close and every day, it was tarnished around the edges and frayed. Sasha and I argued more than we talked. She was about as interested in motherhood as I was in marriage. The dream was better than the reality.

It was easier to tend to the baby than argue with her. The last time she got up for the morning feeding was when we brought Kia home the day after she was born. If I was twenty this would have made sense, but at forty-four it was downright stupid.

I slipped on my robe and sweats before heading to the nursery. This little house used to be perfect, too, but now Kia's crying bounced off the wall like a drunken alley cat.

She was lying on her back. Her face was scrunched up and real tears streamed into her curly hairline. "What's the matter with Daddy's baby girl?" I picked her up and kissed a salty tear. The wide toothless grin she gave me melted away all the frustration I harbored for Sasha.

Kia was perfect. Her large bright eyes, wet smile, and soft black curls melted my heart. She was the shining spot in my toilet-dwelling life.

I changed her diaper and carried her downstairs. She fussed from her baby seat on the table while I poured formula into the bottle. When it was warm, I cushioned her in my arms, and together we strolled around the small house.

"So what should we do today, little one? Should we try to visit your sister again? I'm sure your mom has something very important to do today that doesn't include us."

Kia tugged on the nipple of the bottle, her eyes growing heavy.

I nestled into the comfy chair in the living room with Kia cradled in the bend of my elbow. She was so small, and even though her coloring was a little darker than Crystal's, the two of them looked so much alike. The moment I laid eyes on Kia, she stole my heart. Right now, she was the glue that held Sasha and me together.

I made this bed and I knew I was supposed to sleep in it. I just had no idea it would turn out like this. The moment I moved in, Sasha stopped talking about marriage. Now that she had the cow and the milk, the need to put a ring on it must have faded, and I wasn't crazy enough to bring up the topic. Since she was only a few years older than Crystal, she must have thought she had plenty of time, or the idea of marrying a man almost twice her age wasn't as appealing as she'd imagined.

I could hear my mother snickering in my ear about my stupidity. I tore my family apart and there wasn't a single day when I didn't think about Tracy.

I could still hear her laugh.

I could still smell her cologne.

I could still feel the way she kissed my earlobe before falling asleep.

And I missed it all. I ached for it.

I must have sat for an hour. Kia was asleep, the bottle was empty, and there was no need for me to go back upstairs. I picked up my cell from the table and dialed Crystal. It was early, but I needed to catch her before she started planning her day.

"Yeah?" Her grumpy salutation warned me to tread easy.

15

"I'm glad I caught you. Don't you want to spend time with me and your sister today?"

"Who is this?"

"How many sisters do you have?" I'm sure she knew who it was. There were times when she was almost civil with me, but I had to catch her in a good mood. Calling before nine in the morning probably wasn't the way to do it.

"With you I'm never sure." She shot back. She was quiet for several seconds. "You know only old people make calls this early on a Saturday morning."

The remark stung more than she could have imagined. A punch would have been less painful.

"Are you free today?"

"No. I've got plans."

"Well, okay. We'll do it another time. Maybe next weekend." I shifted the baby from one arm to the other.

"How's Kia? Is she walking yet? The last time I saw her, she looked like she was ready to take off."

It felt good just talking to Crystal. Only Kia could make her do that. "No. She'll walk around the coffee table holding on, but I can't get her to let go. She's chatting, too, but I can't understand anything she says, so I pretend."

"Oh Daddy, she's growing up so fast. I wish I could spend more time with her. Let's meet in Philly next weekend."

"Sounds good, but I need to check with Sasha."

16

And just like that the connection seemed to go dead. Anytime I mentioned Sasha's name, Crystal withdrew. It was as if she thought Kia and I existed here alone.

"Are you still there?" I asked.

"I'm here. Let me know. Look, I gotta go." She was almost there with me and in a snap she pulled away.

"Before you hang up, do you have a number where I can reach your mother?"

Again dead air hung between us. I could hear birds chirping.

"Why?" She could have been channeling Sasha when I'd told her we couldn't afford a trip to Australia this year. I had to have a really good reason or she'd hang up.

"Some financial papers…I need her to sign." I tried to sound casual. She was the rabbit I didn't want to scare away. After a full minute, she rattled the number off to me. I had to shift Kia to write it down because I knew she wouldn't give it to me again or repeat herself.

I shoved the scrap of paper into my pocket.

"Okay, so we're on for next weekend? If Sasha gives you permission, maybe Kia can stay over both Saturday and Sunday with me. Check with your keeper and let me know."

She always managed to get her dig in. Sometimes they were more painful than others. Today wasn't as bad. She was never going to like Sasha. I needed to accept that hurtful reality. The two of them could have been friends, but never step-mother and step-daughter.

"Who you talking to?" Sasha padded into the living room, sneaking around, spying on me. The short nightie barely covered her round butt. Every time I glimpsed her nakedness or near nakedness, my body had the same reaction. My flesh was weak. If she cocked her finger, I'd be between her legs in seconds.

"Crystal. Why?"

She nodded. "What did she say about me?"

I put Kia in the portable crib and followed Sasha in the kitchen. "We didn't talk about you. She wants to see Kia."

"That's good, right?" She reached up into the cabinet and pulled down a box of cereal, exposing her plump round ass to me.

My morning woody was back. If I played her game, I could get lucky this morning.

"Since she's not working maybe she can take the baby for the whole week, then you and I can go away. I just got an email for a special deal. Four days, three nights in the Caribbean? What do you think?" Her high pitch warned me this was something she really wanted. The smile that she'd used to trap me spread across her face.

I ran my hand under the short nightgown and

gathered her long hair in my hand before kissing the back of her neck. She seldom wore panties, making access to her so easy. If she wanted something, then she was willing to give me something in return. I pushed the nightie above her waist and pulled her closer. With Kia in the other room, I pulled my sweats down, releasing my throbbing penis.

"Here? Now, Walter?" Disgust filled her voice.

"Why not. You used to like starting your day this way. I want something and you want something. Why can't we both be happy?"

I lifted her up on the counter and kissed her. She smelled like tangerines and mangoes, and her mouth tasted like peppermint. Her skin was soft and as smooth as butter. She fondled my rod and I slipped my fingers between her legs. She was already moist. I pulled her hips forward and entered her before she could change her mind or Kia woke up. She was warm. For several seconds I didn't move. All I wanted to do was absorb the feeling, make it last for as long as I could stand it. I squeezed her ass tighter and she began to rotate her hips. Slow at first, drawing me deeper. I lifted her higher so I could move in and out. Sasha pushed her tongue in my mouth, mimicking my movements. It was times like this that made me put up with all the other stuff.

Satisfying Sasha was always easy. She clawed my back. "Come on, Walter. Stop holding back. Give it to me, baby."

19

I wasn't ready for it to end. This treat was so fleeting, I tried to make it last. But her husky voice in my ear was like having her tongue on my pulsing penis. Sasha may have lacked the mother gene, but she could screw me all day long. Her muscles tightened around me as I let go, opening the gates and letting it all rush out, into her.

We held on to each other until we both regained our breath. I could almost believe life was good.

"I'm surprised you didn't turn me away this morning. You really want this trip, don't you?" I rubbed my hands along her thighs, refusing to let her move until she answered my questions. Sasha had a reason for everything I believed she had tiny strings attached to everyone she wanted to control.

Including me.

"Why would you say such a thing? We make love all the time," she said with extra sweetness. "Aren't you getting enough? I'm just trying to be careful, I don't want to tax your heart."

"I'm fine, Sasha. The doctor said to be careful. He didn't say no sex at all. I'm not that old."

"You're twice as old as I am." Even though she laughed, that joke stopped being funny months ago. Maybe that's why she didn't talk about getting married anymore. The age difference was starting to show.

"Oh, don't look so sad. I was only joking with you." She jumped off the counter. "I was serious about asking Crystal to watch Kia while we get away. We haven't been away since she was born. What do you think? We could have sex every day without having to change diapers or stop for feedings. What do you say?" She poured cereal into a bowl and shoved it across the table to me, then she filled a second bowl.

The breakfast of champions.

We crunched in silence for the three minutes it took us to finish the meal.

"Maybe you're right. Some time away might do us good. But before we make any arrangements, let me check my calendar to make sure nothing important is coming up at work."

She jumped up and kissed my cheek. "Thank you, Walter. I knew you'd come through for me. I'm going shopping. You've got Kia, right?"

She was out of the room and up the stairs before I could respond or tell her to stay away from Neiman Marcus and Bloomingdales.

I pulled Tracy's number from my pocket. Every day I thought about her. Tracy, Crystal, and Kia were the threads that held me together. The magic wand that Sasha used to hold over my life didn't take long to fade. I just wish the veil over my eyes had lifted before my marriage spiraled down the drain.

From the living room I could hear the shower running. I dialed Tracy's number, hoping Crystal didn't still feel the need to protect her mother from

21

me.

The phone rang several times before her voice mail chimed in. The sound of her voice stunned me. I'd forgotten how mesmerizing her soft tone could be. I thought of calling again just to hear her voice. Believing I could right the biggest mistake of my life was a constant hope. Stranger things had been known to happen. Didn't I father a baby at the ripe age of forty-two? If I was brave enough to look that incredible feat in the eye, then I could believe Tracy still had enough love for me to take me back.

I wanted to talk to her, and every day that I denied myself such a simple joy only made my need stronger. It was time to raise the stakes.

Chapter Three - Tracy

I tried not to do a lot of comparing between my first marriage and my second, but in my head I couldn't stop subtracting points from my ex for all his shortcomings.

And there were many.

Marco always came out the winner, but in all fairness, Walter hadn't set the bar very high.

One thing my failed marriage taught me was to be more aware of everything in my relationship. Pretending life is hunky-dory comes with some serious side effects. My first marriage striped away my naïveté, and it's a cloak I don't ever plan to wear again. It's a blessing and a curse, but Marco doesn't seem to be bothered by my constant need to question and verify.

My new twitch impacts my marriage, and my relationship with my friends, and my daughter, too. But at least this time around I don't feel the need to please everyone and get their approval. I don't have to try so hard to get the things I want because Marco's only goal in life seemed to be pleasing me. How did I get so lucky?

In our king-size bed, Marco spooned me, resting his chin in the curve of my neck. His whiskers tickled, but I was too turned on to laugh. "If we're going to look at houses today, we have to get out of bed." I reached back and ran my fingers through his hair. He'd decided to grow it longer and when it was wet, it almost reached his shirt collar. The few strands of gray showing didn't bother him and I thought they made him even more handsome.

I backed into him. The length of his body was warm, connecting us in a way that words never could. This was my favorite time of day. When it was just the two of us and the outside world hadn't yet intruded on the intimacy that surrounded us.

"Why are we even looking for a house? This place is just fine," I said.

"Yeah, but our family is growing. We need a place big enough for Bria to come visit, and room for Max and Crystal when they come to town."

I turned on my back to see him. His ability to always think about others had no limits. I placed my hand on his face, running my palm over the stubble on his cheek. In the six months since we'd been married, I think I finally understood the real meaning of love. I no longer had to filter my thoughts and words. It's almost like I'd graduated into my life and there were no more tests to pass.

"What would you say if I asked you to stop taking the pill?" His voice was just a whisper.

"Why would you ask me to do that?"

"Well." He tapped my breastbone with his index finger. "You've heard the saying, new house, new car, new baby. We've got the car. Hopefully this week we'll sign a contract on a house, so it's time to complete the equation."

Baby.

I could pretend I didn't hear him, but he was looking directly into my eyes. Waiting on my reply. "Why would we want to do that? Crystal hasn't said anything to me about starting a family."

"I wasn't talking about Crystal. I was talking about us. I've been toying with the idea of having a baby." He ran his hands down my waist and settled them on my hips. The disadvantage of not always paying attention is that little stuff like this can turn into major life-changing stuff. The trap door that I thought I had left behind creaked open and waved me over.

"Baby. Are you serious?" I barely got the words out. Just in case I heard wrong, I didn't want to plant a seed I wasn't willing to water and watch grow. I cleared my throat even though nothing was clogging it. "We never talked about children. I guess I thought we were both in the same place."

"We always have to be ready for change. I guess I'm just so happy, I want to extend it. I dreamed of raising children, doing homework, going to games, stuff like that. My divorce denied me that chance. With my daughter living in Texas, I'm missing so much. Pictures and videos aren't the same. Now I can get that back."

"You've given this a lot of thought," I said. I wanted to say what woman in her forties wants to start another family.

"I have, but I can see you need a little time to think about it. That's fair." The earnest smile almost demanded I start studying up on the possibility of raising a child when I couldn't Tweet, didn't have a Facebook account, and refused to post pictures on Instagram. The idea of attending parent-teacher conferences again sounded like a life sentence. How could I become a mother again when I was only a few years away from qualifying for my AARP card? Doing that would make me as ridiculous as Walter.

Marco sat up and dropped his legs over the side of the bed. "Let's go look at a house. We have plenty of time to talk about the future."

We dressed, ate, and got in the car with very little conversation. All the talking was going on in my head.

####

Marco turned off the car in front of the tenth house we'd looked at in the last two weeks. Finding a home that didn't contain the ghost of Walter or the small condo he owned before marrying me was our number one goal. This time instead of pushing to get my way on a two-story colonial, I was open to anything, as long as Marco was in it every night with me.

He walked around the car and helped me out.

With his hand around my waist, he looked up at the English Tudor and asked, "So what do you think, *Caro*?"

The lush green grass and the flowerbed were enough for me to submit a bid, but I was being different this time. Instead of running away with what I wanted, I decided to hold back my enthusiasm. I looked at the fact sheet.

"It sounds perfect on paper. It has everything we want, four bedrooms, three baths, a large open kitchen and a fireplace."

He kissed my forehead. I cherished every kiss he gave me. They all seemed genuine and full of love. I kept mental track of every single one. It took me a long time to embrace my new life. Some mornings I woke up thinking it was all a dream and I'd be in bed alone, but then he'd throw an arm over me, pull me against him, and I'd exhale.

"We better get inside, the realtor is waiting on us." He grabbed my hand and led me up the red paver sidewalk. "I have a special feeling about this one," he said.

"Are you sure the feeling you have isn't exhaustion, maybe you're just tired of looking." I nudged him.

"Not at all. This has been fun. Finding the right place for us is important." His wicked grin was enough for me to ask more questions, but the realtor opened the door.

"I was beginning to wonder if you two had changed your mind." She waved us in. "You have all the facts on the house, so I'll let you two look around. If you need me, I'll be in the kitchen. Take your time." Her commission smile grew bigger with the price tag of each house.

The first floor was open and expansive. Just what we wanted. There was even an office to the right of the foyer. It was bigger than we needed, but it looked perfect.

Marco followed me upstairs, grabbing a handful of my ass on the way.

"The master bedroom must be behind those double doors." I wiggled just beyond his grasp and threw open the door.

"Wow, this room is huge. It will fit all the new furniture we plan to buy." He strolled to the bay of windows. "With this southern exposure we'll get the evening sun. Now how romantic is this?"

I swung open the bathroom door. "Oh, you've got to see this. It looks like a spa in here."

Marco nodded. "This is nice."

"It's more than nice. Look at all those showerheads. Can you imagine what we can do in there?" I asked.

He pulled me close and looked in my eyes. "I'll be glad when we make a decision. I think we can be happy in any house. This might be the one. It's plenty big enough. What do you think?"

"Do you really like it?" I know I sounded needy, but some habits are hard to break. I didn't want to be in another relationship all by myself, so I was always including him on every decision. Maybe I was swinging the pendulum too far in the other direction, but I figured it was the safest thing to do.

"Believe me, love, I like it. Let's put in an offer. The sooner we get settled, the sooner we move on with our lives." He pinned me against the wall. "There's a room for my daughter when she visits. There's a room for Crystal and Max when they visit, and even your mother. We can even turn one of the rooms into a nursery if we want."

I had hoped the baby thing was just a whimsical thought. But his earnest tone warned me he was serious. Serious enough for me to pay closer attention.

"Have you been thinking about it? Lately it seems to be the only thing I'm thinking about, beside my sexy wife. We don't have to make a decision right now. I'll give it time to soak in." He pressed against me and his penis throbbed against my thigh. He ran his hand under my shirt. His warm touch made my whole body tingle.

"We can't make love here. The realtor will hear us."

"I don't care. We're married, it's all legal now."

I accepted his tongue, his touch, and I'd accept his baby, too, if it would make him happy.

Chapter Four - Crystal

If I had the ability to control my temper, I would have sat on the small sofa in our small living room and waited for Max to walk through the door so I could emasculate him for standing me up. But I liked the passive aggressive approach. There were so many other evil ways to get back at him. I just had to think of some.

I rushed in the door, hoping I'd beat Max home, which I had. The longer he took to get home, the more I could sulk and nurture my disappointment until it was ripe with indignation. I stripped off the gorgeous dress, leaving it on the floor, and crawled into bed.

I couldn't sleep, but I could pretend. The last thing I wanted to hear was a bunch of apologies. This was one of those transgressions that required at least a two day silent treatment.

In the last six months, he'd given me excuse after excuse, so much so that I could have made money if they were worth anything. Even though I was in my twenties when my parents divorced, I still felt like I was from a broken home, which sent my insecurities to an all-time high.

I was looking for signs of Max's infidelity like I thought my mother should have. She had lived so far off in la-la land, dad could have paraded a stream of women through their house and she would have thought they were there to clean the already immaculate rooms.

Where most people spent their time trying to figure out their next vacation, I was obsessed trying to be unlike my mother.

From the bedroom I heard Max close and lock the apartment door. The thump of his briefcase on the floor was the key to close my eyes and try not to scowl.

"Crystal, are you awake?" His voice was low. I could hear the apology he was dying to provide. There was a scent of roses, too. Not the cheap ones sold at the bodega up the street, but the kind a florist sold that actually smelled like the flowers in my grandmother's garden.

"I'm sorry, honey. I'll make it up to you. I promise." He sounded so sincere I almost gave up my ruse. He must have stood there watching me sleep for several moments, and then I heard him in the kitchen.

The next morning I stayed in bed until he was gone. Which was easy, he left for work so early I didn't have to keep up the sham for long.

Before I could get out of the apartment, my father called.

"Hey, baby girl," he said when I picked up.

"Why are you still calling me that? You have Kia now." I was grumpy, but he had nothing to do with my attitude.

"Yeah, but you were baby girl first. No matter

how old you get, you'll always be that little bundle we brought home from the hospital."

"Yeah, okay. What's up?"

"I was wondering if you could watch Kia for us for a week. Sasha and I would like to get away for a little trip."

"Well…I'd like to spend time with Kia, but…" The thought of doing something to please Sasha twisted my stomach. She had taken my father away.

"Do this for me, Crystal. Sasha and I are having a hard time and maybe if we spend time together, alone, we can fix things."

When Kia was first born, I tried to ignore her. I had so many reasons not to like her and for not wanting to invite her into my life. But finally, having a sister was far more consuming than all the negative stuff my parents had tried to saddle me with. Besides, with a mom like Sasha and a dad like Walter, she was going to need me. I certainly needed her.

"Sure Dad. I'd love to watch her. I'm doing it for Kia, so don't get it twisted and think I like Sasha."

"Thank you." He exhaled. "I can always count on you."

"Don't try to sweet talk me, Dad, I said I would do it."

"Is your mother in town? I've tried to call her and she's not picking up."

"I'm not going to feed you information on Tracy. If you were so interested in her, you should have stayed married to her." I sounded madder than I was. Mom was too happy now to be denied her new life.

"She pushed for the divorce. I begged her not to do it." His voice was low, as if the pain was still fresh.

"You didn't leave her much choice, did you?"

"Don't forget you're talking to your father. I don't owe you any more explanations. You can be as angry as you want, but it will eat you up. Let it go, Crystal. You'll learn relationships are hard, and deeper than what you see on the surface. I just hope you don't learn it the hard way, like I did." His words were filled with resolution.

We discussed the arrangements for Kia and hung up. It was too late for him to give me fatherly advice. I couldn't look him in the eye anymore. Besides, I had my own problems to deal with.

I found the business card Dexter gave me and dialed him.

"You got Dexter, talk to me," he said when he picked up.

"And you have me, Crystal.' I tried to sound happy. "I want the job, if it's still available. I can start right away, but I'll have to take a few days off. I promised my dad, I'd watch the kid while he and his side piece went away."

"Legs. How are you? What made you change your mind?" He laughed.

"Too much time on my hands."

"Okay, then. It's yours. I'll send over some documents. You'll need to be bonded. I'm glad you're joining our team. If you could see my grin right now, you'd laugh at me."

"My grandfather used to say, always go where you're wanted. And it sounds like you want me."

"Well, you got that right." There was something in his voice that told me this wasn't a good idea, but I ignored the warning. I needed to be in control, and having a job—any job was the only thing I could think of that would make me feel powerful.

After we hung up I tried to busy myself. There is only so much daytime television I can watch, or closets I can clean, or sites I can surf before my mind starts searching for trouble. My thoughts turned to Max. Usually by now he would have called several times, but the phone hadn't rung all day.

I glanced at the old clock above the kitchen sink. It was after four. Without hesitating, I changed out of my sweats and put on a pair of skinny jeans and the highest pair of heels I could find.

In front of the apartment, I jumped into a cab just as someone heading to the bakery climbed out. I gave the driver the address for Max's firm and settled into the seat.

I was always suspicious. My actions were just in case. Just in case Max thought about cheating on me, he'd know I wouldn't put up with the lies and the sneaking.

On our honeymoon we vowed to always be honest, and for the most part I was. But I would have bet anything, even my huge diamond engagement ring, that Max was getting additional thrills outside of our apartment on West 78th Street.

The taxi meandered in and out of traffic. He had no idea I needed to get to Max's office before he left for the day. How else was I going to catch him in the middle of something incriminating?

By the time we pulled into the lot, I was almost calm and sensible, thinking the whole ride down here was a big waste of time. Surely he wouldn't cheat on me. But when I saw him exit the building with a tall blonde, my anger careened out of control. I threw a twenty-dollar bill across the seat at the driver and jumped out of the car.

Making a scene wasn't the reason I came down here. But the two of them laughed as he steered her towards the Town Car that he often used for late appointments. Just before slipping into the back seat she looked up at him. There was a hint of something in her eyes. The same something that I used to give him when I wanted him to tear off my panties and take me.

Fear of being like Tracy pulled me across the lot so fast I almost stumbled in my heels.

"Max?" My voice carried in the spring air like birds in flight.

He turned around. His face registered a warm

smile as if he were happy to hear my voice. I charged forward with my index finger pointed at him. I can only imagine what my face must have looked like. If it mirrored the turmoil raging inside of me, then I must have looked like a recent escapee from the lunatic ward.

His expression changed, turned into a frown, and deepened the wrinkles in his forehead. "Crystal, I wasn't expecting you."

"I can see you weren't. But it looks like I got here at the right time." I tilted my chin toward the blond. She backed up an inch. "So who is this? Is she the reason you didn't make dinner last night or why you didn't have time to call me all day?"

His eyes widened. "Crystal, I don't believe you're doing this. What is wrong with you?" He rubbed his forehead and looked away from me. He turned to the blonde.

"Please excuse me, Rebecca. I'll have the driver take you all the way home and I'll give you a call next week. We should have the investigator's report by then." He closed the car door and gave instructions to the driver.

After the car drove away, he looked at me for several moments as if he didn't know me. There was disappointment in his eyes. The kind that makes toddlers drop their head and wait on the timeout they know is coming.

"Crystal, she was a client. At least, she used to be

if your antics haven't sent her running to another firm." He grabbed my arms and pulled me towards the street. He hailed the first cab that came our way, and climbed in beside me.

He gave the driver our home address and settled back against the seat. With his briefcase at his side and his hands in his lap, he stared straight ahead. His jaws clenched and unclenched, but he said nothing.

"I'm sorry, Max. It's just when you didn't show up last night, I started thinking all kinds of crazy stuff." I sounded less like a mad hatter and more like the sensible person I was capable of being.

"I understand what you've been through. I really do. And I'm sorry your father has hurt you so badly, but I cannot and will not let those things jeopardize my job like it has our marriage." He heaved a heavy sigh that signaled the worst of his speech was yet to come. "We need to take a little time away from each other. I need a break from all your accusations and manic actions."

"No, we don't need to be apart. That will only make matters worse. Are you suggesting it because there is someone else you wanted to be with?" The crazy person inside of me was back. I caught the driver's eye in the rear view mirror.

Max placed his hands over mine and stared at my face. "Crystal, maybe we should find someone to talk to. I've told you hundreds of times, I'm not like your father. I'm not seeing anyone. I'm only working. But nothing I say seems to make you feel any better or trust me more. I'm not prepared to live my life wondering when you're going to fly off into one of your rages or tear into my office accusing me of sleeping with someone there."

Only half of me was listening, the other half was frozen with shock. It's a good thing Max couldn't read my mind. He'd know how screwed up I really was. I used to be daddy's little princess. I could count on him for anything. Now I know he's just another man with faults like all the rest of them. What am I supposed to do now? When your hero is unmasked, it does terrible things to the psyche.

"What are you saying?" I couldn't help yelling at Max. I had to release the pressure or I would have exploded.

"The firm has some condos we use for out of town clients. I'm sure I can stay in one for a few weeks until I can find something more permanent."

"Are you leaving me?" The question came out shrill and hard like the bitter woman I was becoming.

He didn't respond right away. I could almost see him processing the answer, looking for the words to convince the jury that this was in my best interest.

"Crystal, we can't keep doing this to each other. We need someone to help us navigate through this. Would you be willing to go to counseling?"

I drew away from him. Anger flooded all of my senses. I was seeing black, my skin felt hot, and my ears rung with the sound of a thousand church bells. I wanted to slap him, to yell something that would bring him to his knees just like he was doing to me. But my mind spun like a whirlpool. I couldn't grasp anything to throw back at him that would right the situation.

"I'll tell you what we can do. When we get home, get your stuff and get out. I can't stand to look at you right now."

His eyes widened and darkened. He bit his bottom lip. Satisfied that I'd hurt him just like he'd done me, I sat back.

The car pulled up to our apartment and the driver shut off the meter. He was probably happy to have us out of his cab. Walter paid the fare and got out.

"Every man is not Walter Baptiste, Crystal." His words and stare were ice cold. He left me sitting in the car and walked to the entrance of the condo.

Chapter Five - Tracy

Forty-eight hours passed and Marco hadn't mentioned having a baby. I should have been relieved, instead I felt like Marie Antoinette in Place de la Concorde walking toward the guillotine where my head would be chopped off. We picked up the pace of our life, kept it moving. He didn't have to worry about me tipping the balance of our life. I liked it exactly the way it was.

"What time is your dinner with the girls?" Marco looked over his book at me. I liked that he didn't make up rude names for my friends.

"Dinner is at seven. I'm going up to get dressed now." I unfolded my legs and kissed him on the cheek.

"Will you talk with your friends about the elephant in the room?" There was nothing in his tone that should have caused my heart to skip, but it did.

"What elephant?"

"The one with the name tag that reads baby. The one you've tip-toed around for the last two days." His smile was genuine.

"How did you know I planned to talk to them about this? How did—"

He pulled me down on his lap and held me tight. "I pay attention. I know when my baby is happy and I know when she's sad. Right now you seem numb more than anything else. We can always talk about it some more."

Marco asked for so little. He had to be the easiest going man I ever met. To deny him anything felt selfish. I was trying so hard not to tote the baggage from my first marriage into my second, but starting another family was scary.

He kissed my forehead.

"I better get going, I'm already late." I held his face between my palms. "I'm lucky to have you. We've got time to make this decision don't we?"

The light that flickered in his eyes when he pulled me onto his lap dimmed enough for me to notice. "Having a baby means a lot to you, doesn't it?" I caressed his cheek.

"You mean a lot to me. I couldn't be happier. Go to your dinner." He kissed me again and shifted his hips just enough to push me from his lap.

I drove to Carla's house to pick her up. We were meeting Ursula in Glen Mills for dinner. God must have taken the steering wheel from me and maneuvered the car to Carla's house, because I don't remember turning onto Route 896 or exiting onto 95 North. I pulled into the driveway of her Hockessin home. It looked more like an estate with its gray brick and dark gray shutters. Carla insisted she and Javier needed a big place to raise happy children. Before I could get out of the car, she came out. She snapped open the car door and was strapping on her seat belt before I could say hello.

"Let's just go before some more hell breaks loose in that house and Javier comes running out to draw me back in." She jerked back and forth in the seat like I was driving a Flintstone's car and she could get it going with her feet.

"Okay, okay, I'm going. Don't tell me you're complaining about motherhood. You were drooling for this, remember."

She pushed her big hair out of her eye. "Yeah, I just didn't think I was going to get two babies at once. I'm a rookie. Whoever said two is as easy as one was lying. It's been a week since Javier and I had sex. For us that's a severe drought. We give each other long loving looks all night while we're getting the babies ready for bed, but by the time we finally get them asleep, we're too tired or too covered in drool to perform."

"Stop it, girl." I laughed with her. "You're glowing. I don't think I've ever seen you happier."

She shook her head, fully thinking about what I said. "You're right. I just didn't expect all my happiness to come in one basket. But I wouldn't change one single thing. Those babies have taken my heart and I don't think they're ever going to give it back." She looked at me for confirmation.

"You got that right. Sometimes I think Crystal carries my heart around in her handbag. A mother's heart takes a lot of bangs and bumps." It wasn't until I said the words that I knew what I was afraid of. Being a mom was a full-time job. Everything was second to being there when she needed me. Finally, I was getting my chance to live, and Marco was asking me to delay it again. I didn't want to be one hundred before this chance rolled around again.

"Did you hear me?" Carla looked over at me.

"I'm sorry. I was focusing on the traffic."

"I asked what is going on with Ursula. I tried to talk to her yesterday and she was very closed-mouthed."

"I got the same vibe from her. Maybe today, if both of us pounce on her, she'll open up."

"When was the last time you saw Ursula?" I pulled into the lot of P.F. Chang.

"The baby shower. But that's my fault. I've been so busy, most days I don't even comb my hair." She pulled down the visor and checked her appearance in the mirror. Carla always looked pulled together. Her flaming red hair showed no signs of needing a dye job, and her makeup must have been professionally applied. "I was just checking to see if I had any peas on my face or in my hair." She laughed.

I could see Ursula pacing back and forth in front of the entrance. With her arms folded under her chest, she stared at the concrete sidewalk. She was the only black woman I knew that never left the house unless she was fully made up. From the car, I didn't see her signature taupe lip gloss, and her hair was pulled back into a tight ponytail. Something had to be wrong. "Come on. She's waiting."

We went through the formality of the hugs and kisses, but something was missing. The three of us used to see each other at least once a week, now we were scattered like falling leaves. I'd had a hand in the separation, choosing to spend time with Marco, trying to cement our relationship before any cracks could take root.

We were barely seated inside the darkened restaurant before our server showed up. She took our drink orders before talking us into the lettuce wrap appetizers.

Ursula wasn't an emotional woman, but years of friendship told me something in her life wasn't going the way she wanted. The wrinkle between her eyes hadn't eased since we sat down. "Ursula, how can you look so sad and not share it with us?"

She glanced across the table at Carla and me, but for several moments she didn't say anything. My friend was the one who always had advice for everyone. I grew up thinking nothing would ever get her down. Even at ten, when what was supposed to be a normal Saturday morning, her father died of a heart attack. Instead of falling apart and drawing into a shell or rebelling against the world, she only missed one day of Ms. Carter's fifth grade class, and even when she returned, she never seemed beaten by the cruel hand of fate. But today, her flame may not have been extinguished, but one stiff wind would do it in.

"It's Anthony, or I should say, it's our relationship."

Carla leaned across the table. "Okay, what's going on? What did the bastard do?"

Ursula picked up the glass of water and took a long sip. "It's what he isn't doing that's causing the problem. We've had the longest engagement I know of outside of Hollywood. Every time I bring up setting a date, he gets this look like he has just eaten bad sushi and he needs to find the nearest toilet."

"You think he doesn't want to get married now?" I asked.

"Why do you care? You used to drop men if they wore the wrong color shoes with brown pants. Just drop him." Carla had enough indignation for the both of us.

"Carla…" Ursula started, but put her hand over her heart and paused.

I knew that look.

I knew how she felt.

I knew the chance of this ending badly was even higher than she thought.

That was me a few years ago.

"You really love him, don't you?" I reached across the table for her hand, hoping to transfer a little of my joy into her life.

She bit her bottom lip and nodded. "I moved to Philly for him. I gave up the job I loved for him. He made a lot of promises and to this day, I can't tell you why I believed everything he said. Does love make you do stupid stuff?"

"Oh yeah." Carla and I said almost in unison.

"No one knows that better than me." I raised my right hand. I took the oath that every woman takes the day she gets married, thinking life is going to be like the fairy tales we grow up on. All we need to do is believe. No one believed more than I did or tried harder than me, and still my marriage crumbled. Would it happen again? If I stood my ground and told Marco I didn't want any more children, would I be sending our relationship on a death spiral?

Our appetizers arrived. Even though the aroma made my mouth water, I didn't reach for the biggest lettuce leaf I'd seen in weeks. Trouble surrounded the table and this wasn't the time to think about food.

"You know, I realize I wouldn't be as sensitive to some of his antics if it weren't for Walter. My senses are more acute, just waiting for a sign." She tapped her index finger on the table. With each word she grew a bit angrier.

She was still mad at Walter for me. That's the kind of friend she was. But she needed to let it go. I had.

"That's no reason to be mad at Walter. Maybe we ought to thank him for unveiling the truth of infidelity. At least the three of us will always be wiser now," said Carla.

"He's got a few more weeks to pull his act together or I'm leaving. I'm not one of those girls who puts up with bullshit."

"Ursula, please don't let what happened to me influence your relationship. Anthony may have some very good reason for his behavior, and it might not have anything to do with another woman. Just confront him. Don't wait for the anvil to land on your head before you see the real world."

Our meals showed up before we'd even touched the appetizers. A few years ago, I would have gobbled everything in sight and impatiently waited on more to show up. Food used to massage my internal demons. Eating my feelings was better than examining them closer.

I couldn't let Carla and Ursula get away without telling them about Marco's ridiculous request. While we waited for the server to return with our check, I took a deep breath and jumped right in.

"Marco wants to have a baby." Saying it aloud made it sound more absurd. My statement hovered over the table like a ship from outer space.

Carla looked at me, then at Ursula. Ursula tilted her head like I'd only given her part of a story and there was more to come.

"That's it, ladies. Aren't you guys going to say something? Aren't you going to tell me how stupid that is or how stupid you think Marco is?"

"As handsome as that Italian stud is, I'd have

a baby for him." Carla laughed.

"You just like the idea of being pregnant," Ursula said.

"I was only kidding. I don't care about Marco. I only care about you. What do you think? What do you want?" Carla took a sip of her soda, and then pushed the empty glass into the middle of the table.

I turned to Ursula. "Aren't you going to say something?" I asked.

She shook her head. "I think Carla asked some good questions. Answer her first and then I'll weigh in."

We hadn't eaten dessert, but my spoon was still on the table. I flipped it over two times without saying a word. If I really knew what I wanted, the big knot sitting in the bottom of my stomach wouldn't exist.

"I love Marco. I love him more than I loved Walter, and I used to think the sun and moon revolved around Walter. So that should give you an idea of what I'm talking about. But having a baby now for me would be like going backwards. I just got rid of the twenty pounds of baby fat I gained with Crystal. I don't want to do midnight feedings, or playdates, or first birthday parties at Chucky Cheese, or teething, or chicken pox, or running noses or—"

Carla held up her hand. "You just described my life, so go easy. There's no need to disparage the reality I'm living." She leaned close enough for me to

48

see her mascara was smudged, giving her the appearance of tiny black eyes. "Besides, all those things are great. I actually look forward to the late night feedings. The house is quiet and I get to spend quality time with the babies."

"If it was so great, why did you fuss all the way to the restaurant about not having sex and not sleeping?" I asked.

"Not because I'm unhappy, that's for sure. I've never been happier. There isn't one single thing about the past sleepless year I would give up. Nothing."

I turned to Ursula. "Your turn, Ursula."

"Haven't you learned to follow your own counsel, yet? No matter what we say or don't say, the final decision is yours. That's the only thing that's going to make you happy."

"But don't you think it's crazy of him to even want a baby?"

"Did you ask him that question?" Ursula asked.

"He said he wants us to be a family. His daughter is in Texas, Crystal is grown, and he said something about us sharing that experience, together."

"Have you talked to your doctor about having a baby? You're not exactly a spring chicken." Ursula's sour expression let me know what she thought of the idea.

49

I pulled my hair behind my ears. "No. He only just brought it up a few days ago. But I do have an appointment next week. Maybe she can give me some advice. Maybe she'll tell me I'm way past the baby stage but to have fun trying." I wasn't as perky as my voice sounded, but I pulled it off. No need to further dampen the mood of our dinner.

They both stared at me, as if I was supposed to say something more profound. "If I say no I'm afraid guilt will eat me up. Or one day he'll get resentful for denying him this."

"Didn't you two talk about this while you were dating?" Carla asked as if she were a dating counselor talking to a teenage girl who didn't have a clue about relationships.

"Back then, I thought we had more important things to talk about. We're not twenty. I guess I thought kids were off the table and we'd moved on to bigger stuff like houses, big trips, and just being happy. I was so focused on being happy I forgot about reality."

Chapter Six - Crystal

At least I didn't have to stare at the four walls in the gloomy condo all day. The job with Dexter wasn't anything to get all excited about, but I was. It got me away from home and gave me a legitimate reason to stare at Dexter all day. The empty side of the closet where Max used to hang his custom suits and his huge collection of designer jeans stomped on my sense of security. It was like living in a rubber raft during rough seas with no end on the horizon. I knew our marriage was going to have some challenges, but I never imagined Max would leave me. I always thought if things didn't work out I'd be the one walking out on him, because I watched everything and listened for signs my marriage was in trouble.

Maybe he was only trying to teach me a lesson. But night after night, I watched the clock, hoping to hear his key in the door. And every morning I woke up alone, feeling rejected and raw, still waiting for my stalled life to restart.

But no matter what, I wouldn't put up with infidelity. I didn't have the forgiving gene. Tracy must have kept it all for herself, knowing she was going to need it.

I climbed out of bed before the hurt overwhelmed me and the tears started. Again.

If there was someone who would understand what I was going through it was my godmother. Ursula was

51

old enough to be my mother, but she never acted like one and no matter what I did or said, she was always on my side. It was like having a favorite blanket whenever I needed one. She was the only person who never delved too deep to find out the root cause. For Ursula life was simple—black and white. It was as if her only responsibility as godmother was to make sure I had a safety net if I fell and a shoulder to cry on any time I needed it. And I needed it now a lot. Married life was nothing like I dreamed it would be. It felt more like a job with a field full of land mines. One day we were going along, happy and wonderful, and the very next moment something so minor that it shouldn't have mattered blew up in my face. Instead of having a lovely dinner with my husband, I found out my life was full of deception that I refused to ignore.

All those romance books that had shaped my courtships promised flowers, decadent dinners, unexpected trips, and love-making so wicked the sheets caught fire. But my happy ending hadn't unfolded. Right after the honeymoon my make-believe world had collided with my real one and nothing had been right since.

I dialed Ursula's number.

"What's wrong? You sound unhappy," she said after I greeted her.

I stalled for a moment. The only person who knew any details of all my problems was Dexter. The moment I told Ursula, the tarnish on my marriage would be exposed to the light.

"It's Max…I mean it's Max and me." I heard the strident sound of my voice, but having to admit I was part of the problem was like a kick in my gut. "He moved out."

"Did you say he moved out—as in left you? What happened?" Her indignation bolstered me. She was on my side.

"He said he was working late. But when I showed up at his office he wasn't there. No one was there. And a few days later I caught him walking out of his office with a tall pretty blond." I laid out the details, trying to keep the incrimination out of my voice. When I reached the end of my story, I was exhausted. Drained.

"That rat bastard. What do you think is going on? That's a lot of coincidences for him to explain. What did he say when you asked him?" Her questions ran together in a high-pitched yell.

"He says I'm overreacting. That he's not like Walter." I spit the words out, saying them left a bad taste behind.

"Huh, then he ought to stop acting like him," Even though she mumbled, I heard what she said.

"So you think I'm right?" I bounced in my seat as if she was giving me something to celebrate. It took two seconds for me to understand the weight of her words. How could a love so pure and optimistic die so fast?

"You need to find out for sure. Once you do, make a decision and stick with it. I don't like the idea that he moved out. If he wasn't guilty, why would he do that?"

"I think he's hiding something." I said with more self-righteousness than I should have. With Ursula I could be as snarky as I wanted.

"All this talk about me and I haven't asked about you and Anthony. How are you? How's Anthony? Have you guys set a date yet?"

"Don't ask. No date yet." Her voice went flat. I'd obviously asked questions she didn't want to discuss.

We hung up, but not before she promised to help me if I needed her, and not to tell my mom about me and Max. I wanted to be the one to share that horrible news.

I dressed with care. The job was only for an assistant, which meant I answered phones and tracked appointments. No matter how he described it, that's all I was going to do. He couldn't fool me. But my sheer shirt and low slung jeans made me feel sexy. Sexier than I needed to be.

I wasn't trying to entice Dexter, but it felt good thinking I could. Knowing someone just might want to look at me and have lustful ideas of what they wanted to do to me.

I arrived in front of the office. It was a store place. I looked up the address on my phone just to be sure I was in the right place. I had no idea Dexter had an actual place. I expected to be working in his apartment at a desk shoved in a corner that was also used for a table when he wanted to eat. I opened the door and far off in another room I heard a bell chime.

"Ah, you're almost right on time." Dexter rushed toward me with a big grin on his face. I felt like the winner of the Publisher's Clearinghouse Sweepstakes, not an employee showing up for a job that barely paid more than minimum wage. "I was beginning to think you'd flaked out on me."

Dexter was one of those men that found his good looks without even trying. His jet black hair was always tousled to perfection, making me wonder if he did it on purpose or if his curls just knew what formation played up his leading man look. His clothes weren't designer fancy, but the way they fit his well-toned body made them look custom stitched for him, even his jeans.

"I got a little turned around, missed the subway stop." I placed my purse on top of a small desk situated in the middle of what was a colorful showroom.

On the far wall, above the sofa was a painting that resembled the one Max and I had purchased from Dexter to hang over our bed. The abstract had similar colors, but the design was exactly the same. I walked over to get a closer look at the mirrored twin of the picture I'd made love under during those first few months of marital bliss. From some angles I'd had so many orgasms while staring at Dexter's signature I could have forged his name on his blank checks.

The wall behind the picture was the same color blue as my bedroom. An eerie chill crawled up my spine. Was all this just a coincidence?

I turned around to face Dexter. "I thought you were a house painter. You know, the kind who wears white coveralls splattered with paint with a bunch of stir sticks poking out of the pockets."

He laughed. A deep belly racket that sounded sincere. How could he be happy with so much unhappiness swirling around?

"I guess you expected me to have a piece of straw stuck between my teeth, too." His hands encompassed the room. "Can't you tell by the amazing work I did on your condo that I'm not an ordinary house painter. I like to make special things of ordinary things. Now you'll get to see my craft up close and in person."

He pulled out the simple chair behind the desk. I took the seat. He pushed another straight back chair across the room and placed it beside me. He sat so close I inched away just enough to feel comfortable.

"Let's start with the scheduling software I use. Then we'll move to the colors, the ordering, and managing the crew." He switched into serious mode. I'd never seen this side.

"You have a crew?" My voice was syrupy sweet and I leaned a little closer to him.

"I don't usually paint homes, but I couldn't resist the temptation of getting to know you."

I nodded. "And the picture?" I pointed to the painting on the other side of the room.

"I wanted to leave something personal behind." He looked directly in my eyes as if there was something more he was going to say.

Words escaped me, so I nodded again. The intense stare he gave me said enough. "We better get started," I said, breaking the trance.

It was important for me to concentrate. I couldn't let my thoughts roam one inch to the right or left. I had to focus on what was in front of me or I'd start to feel the empty hole in my heart. I stared at the computer and tried to absorb everything Dexter said.

The hapless jogger and painter I thought I knew was really quite organized, creative, and more driven than I thought. He didn't just paint walls. He painted murals, portraits, and masterpieces. He was scheduled to paint the portrait of some corporate executive later in the week. Even though he wasn't specific, I got the impression he was going to be paid six figures for one sitting. His nonchalance over all of it was intriguing, and perked my interest.

All of this should have been great news, but as long as I thought he was a struggling hack, a step away from being the man living under the Brooklyn Bridge in a box, he could be the fantasy in my head. And only in my head.

But he was real and strong and powerful. With big, muscular arms powerful enough to wrap around me and tell me my life was going to turn out okay.

The morning passed in a blur of his testosterone and training and discussions on color shades I didn't even know existed. I was breathless and exhausted by the time my stomach started to growl.

"Okay, I heard that. You're hungry and it's time to take a break. The last thing I want is for you to pass out on your first day of work. Come on, my treat. It's one of the benefits of working here."

I grabbed my purse. "You buy lunch every day?"

"I'm not here most days. But if I happen to be around at lunch time then you can betcha I'll buy you lunch." He winked.

I forced Max out of my head. He'd walked out on me and the last thing I planned to do was sit home and pine for him. I may be Tracy's daughter, but I was no doormat. I saw myself being more like Ursula. When one relationship didn't work out, then it was time to move on. Dexter looked like a good place to move to.

####

Unlike Delaware, the fun part of living in Manhattan was the ability to walk to lunch, dinner, and almost anywhere. Dexter and I headed up East Houston Street. The weather was perfect and there aren't many perfect days in spring, either it's too cold or the rain moves in to coax spring flowers out of the ground. Of course, there were no beautiful informal gardens for me to admire, unless I counted the small patches of land in front of a few condos where the owner planted four or five tulips to admire.

"Is this okay with you?" Dexter opened the door to a small restaurant nestled just off Houston.

"It looks perfect. What's the specialty?" I hoped he didn't hear the falsetto sound of my voice. I recognized it as nerves, but I didn't want him to detect my insecurity.

"They have the best burger in town and the French fries are always hot, fresh and delicious. My goal is to feed you good food so you'll be a happy employee."

We were seated at a table near the front of the eatery. The crisp linen tablecloths and elegant wine glasses gave the place a more elegant appearance than the casual menu revealed.

The server appeared immediately and Dexter ordered a bottle of Chardonnay. He quickly convinced me I wanted the same entrée he was having for lunch.

"Do you normally have such a luxury lunch, with a whole bottle of wine instead of just a glass?"

"Let's just say I enjoy life and I make time for what's important." His voice was dreamy sexy.

Dexter touched my shoulder and ran his index finger along my forearm. In an instant, beads of sweat broke out on my back.

I was walking into trouble and I knew it. But resentment gurgled in my stomach and every time I thought I was getting better, a new wave washed in. Max had left and nothing said he was coming back. Suppose he didn't. If I hadn't spent a week alone in my bed with no word from him, then maybe I wouldn't have felt like I could do anything I wanted.

The bottle arrived. He waved away the server and poured it himself. He was transforming into a leading man by leaps and bounds right before my eyes.

"So, tell me about the stuff that qualifies as important in your life?" I asked before taking a sip from my glass.

He tilted his chin just a bit. "Let's see, I'm excited about my work and the things it affords me. The travel, the great food, and a nice place to live in a city I love." He raised his glass to mine and took a swallow. "Tell me what gets you out of bed in the morning?"

"Oh, that's not fair. You already know I've been looking for a job for months without any luck. You know Max and I live in a place that would fit into a corner of your studio."

"Yeah, I know those things, but what I don't know is what you want. Do you want a job or a career? Would living in a bigger place make you smile?"

I emptied my glass and he refilled it. "I didn't

know we were going to spend lunch examining my life. You're asking me questions I haven't thought about."

The server reappeared with our entrees. For a few moments we ate in silence, which was probably best since all of a sudden I couldn't think of anything to say. Today wasn't the day for a deep examination of my life. It was in a death spiral and no amount of talk was going to breathe life back into it. Talking about Max would have turned on my tear facets and nobody wanted to hear me babbling about my misfortune.

"So what do you think so far about the job? Do you think you will stick around?"

"I'm really quite impressed. I had it in my head that you were too laid back to really be a successful businessman." I measured my words because the wine had released all the restraints I normally put on my observations. Dexter was handsome and I'd seen his power every time we ran together. His arms were well sculpted. Seeing him in his natural habitat revealed a depth I couldn't have known existed. He was getting sexier with each glass of wine and I was getting less inhibited.

"Why is that, because I didn't brag enough? Or did you judge me by the clothes you saw me in, workout wear and painting attire?" He smiled, but I think my comment surprised him.

I shrugged a shoulder. "What did I know? You have a quiet way about you."

"There's a lot of stuff going on under this quiet exterior." He refilled my glass, then his. The bottle of wine was almost gone and so was everything that held me grounded. With Max out of the apartment I wasn't just lonely, I was flapping in the wind.

By the time lunch was over, my plate was clean. The food was as good as Dexter promised and the second bottle of wine was half empty.

"It's a good thing we're walking, huh?" I said to Dexter as we headed back to his store.

"Now you know my secret for staying fit. I eat whatever I want and I walk it off. And what I don't walk off, I find other ways to work it off." He whispered in my ear. His nose brushed my ear. I think it was innocent, but I still tingled.

The way his hand rested on my waist was just as intimate. We had to look more like a couple than two co-workers heading back to the office. Married women shouldn't have the thoughts which were clogging my head right at that moment. Every time Dexter touched me, it was like a sexual signal waking up some part of my body that I had forgotten existed, preparing it for something so forbidden, it made my knees shake just thinking about it.

He unlocked the door to the studio and pulled me into his arms. I didn't resist. Maybe I didn't want to or maybe I was getting back at Max, but when he kissed me, I let him. His lips were sweet. He pressed his tongue into my mouth. A warm feeling rushed up my back and settled in the pit of my belly.

His tongue wiped away every thought of Max. For the first time in a long time, I was only thinking about myself. It was both decadent and freeing, and I just wanted to release the restraints confining me. A place where I seemed to be all alone. Max had his work and whatever else kept him entertained. Mom had Marco, and Dad had another whole family. I didn't fit in anywhere.

The moment was mine. Having Dexter kiss me was my revenge on Max for cheating and then leaving me. Even though he couldn't see me, just knowing it would hurt him was satisfaction enough. Dexter didn't want anything from me but sex. The idea was as exciting as it was foreign.

He cupped my breasts through the thin shirt before inching down inside my jeans. His movements were slow, allowing time to draw me in, erasing all the inhibitions clogging my thoughts. He slipped his finger inside of me without releasing my tongue. I should have held him tighter, or attempted to unbutton his shirt or reached for his penis. But I couldn't. As long as I let him do all the probing and disrobing, guilt didn't assault me and make me want to run away like a high school virgin. I felt less culpable.

Dexter led me to the sofa. He loomed over me and pushed my blouse above my breasts. Then he unbuckled my belt and pulled my pants and panties down. When I was naked, he pulled off his shirt exposing a chest more magnificent than I had words to describe. His gym membership was worth every penny. He ran his index finger from my throat down between my breasts, leaving a trail of burning flesh. When he inserted his finger in me, I lifted my hips to meet him.

That's when I saw it.

The painting.

The signature.

Only it wasn't Max stroking that tender spot that was inside the bounds of my marital vows.

I grabbed his hand.

Halting him.

"Do you want me to stop?" His voice was low and husky and I felt like we were already making love.

My mind knew right from wrong but my body craved him. The fantasy in my head took on a vibrancy that sparked my desire.

"Yes. No. I don't know." I rubbed my forehead.

"Let me help you." He laid me back on the sofa and inserted his tongue in my mouth again. This time he was gentler, more caring. His touch was deft, easing away my doubt while ushering in my lust.

I wrapped my hand around his neck and pulled him closer. With excruciating slowness he kissed every part of my neck. And each one turned my body temperature up another degree. I was on fire. This wasn't cheating. It felt too good to be wrong. Max walked out. At this moment, he could be buried between the legs of the blond.

Dexter stripped off my clothes, allowing me to help him. He removed his clothes and towered over me. If I thought his body was great with clothes on, I was amazed at the beauty of his nakedness.

I pushed thoughts of Max aside, just like he'd pushed me aside. I waited anxiously while Dexter rolled on the condom. He lowered his head between my legs and kissed me there. It was so light and tender, at first I thought I had imagined it. But he did it again and my doubt disappeared. He darted his tongue in and out of me as if he wanted to make me climb the walls.

I didn't want to say anything. I didn't want to introduce reality to my fantasy. Dexter seemed to only want to please me and he was good at it. He kissed his way up my stomach and circled his tongue around each breast before entering me.

The connection between the two of us was so intense I had to hold back the orgasm. Sex with Max had become so ordinary, I could predict what he was going to do and when.

Was this better because it was forbidden?

Was this better because it exceeded my fantasy?

Was this better because it was a strike against Max?

Dexter murmured my name, repeating it so many times it sounded like he was making a song of it. He lifted his head and stared down at me. "You can't imagine how long I've wanted to do this."

"Was I worth waiting for?"

"God, yes," he said, and pushed deeper into me.

I closed my eyes and blocked out a vision of Max that was trying to steal away my moment of joy. I wrapped my legs around Dexter, staying in the moment and allowed the pleasure to wash over me in what felt like an endless rush of waves. Maybe the illicitness was the aphrodisiac that I was chasing. The orgasm swaddled me with such euphoria I thought I was going to faint.

The narrow sofa didn't allow enough room for Dexter to roll off of me. He shifted his weight just enough to allow me to catch my breath. He pulled off the condom and dropped it on the floor, then rested his hand on my upper thigh. Even at rest it felt sexual.

With Max I would have rolled over and fallen asleep, but it was the middle of the day and the pressure of Dexter's throbbing penis on my thigh tempted me.

I reached for him.

He stopped my hand, not allowing me to stroke him. "Let me get another condom."

"No. I don't want to wait," I said. If he left me alone, guilt would consume me, making everything sordid. For now, I just wanted to be happy. Even if it was only for the balance of the afternoon. Tomorrow was enough time to think about the consequences.

Chapter Seven - Walter

The expansive lobby of the hotel was packed with college coeds. I had expected more opulence since Sasha had picked it, but she must have been drawn to the spring break crowd instead.

Sasha and I were the only people in the registration line. She looked fabulous. The tiny sundress hugged her breasts and butt, making it impossible for me to stop eyeing her. The young guys at the bellhop desk must have had the same reaction because they turned completely around.

"Did you have to wear that dress? Every man we've passed has ogled you. If I was charging for each look, I could have paid for this trip." I stepped behind her, trying to shield her butt from view.

She batted her long lashes and pressed against me. "You used to like it. Every time I wore it, you said it turned you on."

"Yeah, but since you've had Kia you have more curves and you're filling out that dress in ways you didn't before. It should be illegal." I brushed my lips against hers.

The clerk behind the desk handed me the keys and pointed to the elevator that would take us to our room. I placed my hand on the base of Sasha's back, the men needed to know she was with me. Taken. They needed and to look elsewhere.

"Excuse me, ma'am, you dropped this." A tall dark haired man that had his eyes glued to Sasha's ass ran up behind us. He held the white silk scarf that I recognized as Sasha's laced through his fingers.

"Yes, it is. Thank you so much." Sex dripped from her voice. The last time I heard that tone was before Kia was born.

Maybe it was jealousy, but I would have bet the price of the trip that he touched her hand longer than he needed to hand it over.

We rode the elevator up to our room in silence. I nursed my irritation by clamping my jaw tight. Sasha nursed her happiness by grinning all the way to the room. She was too young and uncomplicated to hide her pleasure for the attention.

In the room, she reached behind her back and unzipped her dress. "Are you happy now, I've taken off the damn dress."

"Take off your bra, too, and then I just might forget that man was flirting with you right in front of me."

She unhooked the bra and dropped it on the floor. "Poor baby. You should be honored. You're in the room with the hot chick, he's not." She unbuttoned my polo shirt and pulled it over my head. Just as swiftly, she undid my belt buckle and pants.

"Call downstairs and ask them to give us a few minutes before bringing up our bags."

I picked up the phone to make the call, but before

the connection was complete she dropped to her knees in front of me and took my rod in her mouth. Somehow I managed to complete the conversation before my knees buckled.

She could do things with her tongue that had to be illegal in several states. The handsome younger man in the lobby was probably the person she pretended she was giving head to, but it didn't matter as long as I was getting the benefit. If I wasn't so addicted to all the sexual tricks she could do to my body, I probably wouldn't have let Tracy walk out of my life. I may not have loved Sasha as much as I loved Tracy, but I worshipped our sex life.

If I was going to be trapped in a loveless relationship, at least the coitus made it worthwhile.

Her final swirl around the tip of my penis was the tipping point. I couldn't hold back another minute. I held her head still and let go of any frustration clinging to me over the lobby incident.

She fell across the bed with me.

"Now that's the way to start a vacation." I whispered in her ear.

"I know how to please my man, don't I?"

"You got it, baby."

She walked her fingers down my chest and around my limp dick. "I remember when you could get another boner almost immediately." Her disappointment was also an accusation on my age.

"Give me a minute. I'm not a machine."

She jumped up, placed her right foot on the bed, giving me a clear shot between her legs. "You used to be. Maybe it's time for you to talk to the doctor about those little blue pills."

"I don't have erectile dysfunction. I just need a couple of minutes." I closed my eyes. If the incident in the lobby didn't swallow my ego, then being demanded to perform and coming up short was enough to do the job.

"Forget it, Walter." She pulled her bikini from her carry-on bag and put it on. "You rest. I'm going to the beach. Once you catch your breath, come on down." Her tone didn't make the invitation sound genuine. She slipped on a bathing suit cover and left the room.

Instead of languishing in the ecstasy I deserved, I took a cold shower, pulled my trunks from the same carry-on and rushed to catch up with her. Our vacation wasn't off to a good start.

Trying to find the beach was easy enough. All I had to do was follow the steady stream of bikini-clad bodies heading outside. If Sasha's words didn't make me feel ancient, just watching the young, lean, active bodies did the job. This was to be my life, always comparing to see if I measured up to some new standard. One day I would fail that test and that thought only confirmed my decision to connect with Tracy.

I had to shield my eyes against the sun. In my hurry, I'd forgotten my sunglasses. There was a sea of green and blue of loungers surrounding the pool. Sasha could have been in any one of them. I had to look like a dope trying to find her.

There were plenty of attractions for me to stop and admire as I cruised the deck around the pool. Firm butts and voluptuous breasts accompanied with tiny waists seemed to be everywhere. I could have easily passed for the father of most of these people. My stomach was still flat, but the muscles that used to define my abs had gone into hiding.

Finding Sasha would have been easier if I had thought to look for the young guy who seemed to think my girl was on the market. He sat on the foot of her lounger, gazing at her breasts while she explained something with her hands. Unless he was talking about the size of her breasts, then he was only pretending to hear her. The way the sun caught her thick hair was pure beauty. She had the kind of looks that made you stare, sometimes with your mouth open, just like Young Guy was doing now.

"Excuse me." My voice was deeper than usual and just as threatening as I wanted it to sound. Young guy jumped up, looking like he'd been caught groping her prized possessions.

"Hey man, I was just telling Sasha about the party we're having in the Black Bay Lounge tonight. Maybe you two can make it." His invitation sounded about as genuine as a used car salesman unloading a lemon.

"We just might see you tonight." Sasha leaned forward, exposing more cleavage than I even knew she had. I couldn't compete with Young Guy. His vigor had more power than money could buy.

Young Guy bounced away, happy with her answer. I flopped into the empty chair beside Sasha. I'm not the jealous type. Never had been. I didn't like losing or sharing either, but I loved a challenge.

Sasha knew how to push my buttons, sometimes I let her, and sometimes I just cut off any emotions. I was in this relationship, committed to this relationship, and no young pup was going to take what was mine. I wasn't going to do to Kia what I did to Crystal.

"Are you having fun?" I placed my hand on the upper part of her thigh. A signal just in case anyone else wanted to give her a test drive.

"Yeah, this is so much fun. Aren't you glad we came?" She spoke while her eyes followed Young Guy across the deck.

"I feel like a chaperone on spring break." And I sounded like a grump, too.

I wish I had a good book or magazine to settle back with, but that would have only marked me for the old man that I felt like. Almost everybody had a pair of ear buds jammed in their ears even though Hip-Hop music blared from a distant speaker. I sighed and settled in for a long trip.

The gradual shifting of the sun made the heat

impossible. I tried to maneuver my chair into a sliver of shade. Never was I going to admit I couldn't handle it. The hotter it got the more Sasha's skin seemed to glow. If the thermometer inched up to one hundred degrees she'd probably shine like a bronze statue. I was willing to instantly combust before I'd leave her alone for Young Guy to come sniffing around her again like a hound in heat.

This woman was going to kill me.

"We have a dinner reservation at seven." I made a show of looking at my watch. "We better head up and get ready."

She didn't think I saw her, but before she stood up she looked in Young Guy's direction. Their eyes locked for less than three seconds, but it was enough. I'd seen that look before, it's the one she used to lure me away from Tracy.

####

Maybe I wasn't the best looking guy in the hotel, but I had to be amongst the few with pockets so deep I could afford the five star restaurants with the over-priced entrees. The dress and shoes Sasha wore to dinner set me back one thousand dollars. She looked sinful. Having her on my arm tonight boosted my ego ten percentage points. For a guy fighting middle age, she was my secret weapon.

Sasha and I sat sipping cognac after our five

course meal while I waited for my food to digest.

She handled the glass candle globe like it was dangerous, tilting it from side to side, running wax over the shiny glass.

"You seem distracted tonight. Is everything okay? Are you missing Kia?"

She looked up at me. "No. I'm sure she's fine with Crystal." She placed her napkin on the table. "Maybe we should head up. Aren't you ready to turn in?"

Music to my ears. If she was ready to go to the room then that meant she was ready for a hot night.

"It's only nine. Don't tell me my party animal wants to call it a night already," I said.

"Well, I was thinking…" She rolled her tongue across her lips. "We could go upstairs and finish what we started earlier today. You owe me, don't you?"

"Let's go, baby." I signed the check and escorted her out.

In the room, I kicked off my shoes and undid my belt. I reached for the remote to turn on the television.

"What are you doing?" She hadn't budged from the entrance. "Why are you turning on the television?"

"The play-offs are on. I wanted to catch the tail end of the game. It's only ten minutes left in the final quarter."

"Ten minutes in basketball is like an hour in real time." She could have been a three-year-old and the pout completed the look.

"Fix yourself a drink, it will be over before you know it."

"I can get five drinks for the cost they'll charge us for using the mini-bar." She twisted her hands. "I'll go downstairs and get one in the bar. I'll nurse it slow and by the time I'm done, the game will be over, too. I'll be right back." She tucked her purse under her arm, spun around and left.

I placed my feet up on the sofa and stared at the television. There was always a backstory with Sasha. She didn't any more want a drink than I wanted the Lakers to beat the Bulls. But I pretended I didn't know she went downstairs to hang out with Young Guy, and she pretended not to notice the age difference between us. I'm slowing down and she's in high gear.

I pulled my cell from my pocket and dialed Tracy. She picked up on the second ring.

"Hi, Tracy, it's me, Walter. I didn't catch you at a bad time, did I?"

"How did you get my number?" She sounded more curious than angry, a good sign.

"Crystal."

"What do you want?" she asked.

"Can we have lunch one day next week? I have something I'd like to talk with you about."

Several seconds ticked by and she said nothing. For a moment, I thought the call was disconnected.

"Are you still there?"

"Whatever you want to say, why can't you just say it now?"

"I'd rather talk to you in person. We can have lunch at your favorite place on the River Front. My treat. What do you say?" I knew I was begging, but she sounded so close to saying no.

"I guess I can do that," she finally said.

"Okay. Thanks. How about Wednesday at noon. I'll make a reservation."

"This better be important, Walter, because I can't think of one thing you need to say to me that you can't say over the phone." There was an edge to her voice.

"Thanks, Tracy. See you next week." I ended the call before she could back out.

With a big grin on my face, I turned up the volume on the game and got comfortable. True love never dies, which meant I still had a chance of getting my old life back.

I woke up an hour later, the game was over. I had no idea who won. The local news blared a story about an upcoming flower show. From the large doors leading to the balcony I could see the moon sitting just above the horizon. But, Sasha was nowhere in sight. Which was probably for the best so she didn't witness the dribble on my chin.

I stood up, stretched, and contemplated what to do. All I could think about was Young Guy and peeling him off the mother of my child. I slipped on my shoes, picked up the room key card, and made my way to the lobby.

Chapter Eight - Crystal

I stood in the sunny yellow kitchen waiting on the kettle to boil. It felt strange being in Delaware and not at my mother's house. I never thought I'd step foot in my father's den of iniquity, but making love to a man who's not my husband set my unbalanced world on a strange new course. I couldn't look down my nose at my father from my superior height since I'd taken such a major tumble.

If everything went as planned, I could enjoy a cup of tea before Kia woke up, demanding attention. Deep down, I wanted her to wake up early and keep my mind off of the big problem bearing down on me.

I couldn't stop thinking about Dexter.

I couldn't stop thinking about how he kissed me.

I couldn't stop the images of us on his sofa, on the floor, and finally in his bed. It wasn't until I was in the car he'd called to drive me home that the reality hit me. Coming to babysit for Walter was as far away as I could get.

My thoughts hopped all around the topic. It was almost like I had ADHD, I shifted my focus for a few minutes, but I always returned right back to being in Dexter's bedroom with him between my legs. Loving every minute of it.

How could I have allowed Dexter to touch me, to kiss me? To make love to me? How could I have like it so much? I loved Max. It was just three words and I knew they were true. Which made it impossible to believe I could have done what I did.

I was so worried about being a doormat like my mother, it turns out I was more of an adulterer like my father.

I ran to the trashcan and brought up nothing but bile from my empty stomach. The memory of Dexter's hands where they shouldn't have been and my lust for him wouldn't fade.

Staying at Walter's and Sasha's was like crossing the demilitarized zone. Not only was I betraying the promises I made to myself about setting foot in Sasha's house, but if my mother knew, she would most certainly think her daughter had betrayed her, too. Being here was the beginning of my pittance, until I came up with something more fitting.

It was almost six. I picked up my cell phone to dial Max, but it rang before I could make the call. It was Dexter. His fourth call in two days. All the messages were the same. "What happened? Call me." Just looking at his illuminated number made my neck warm.

"Yes, Dexter." My tone wasn't warm or friendly. I needed to put some distance between us.

"Finally. Have you been getting my messages?" The deep quality of his voice was enough to weaken my resolve.

"Yes."

"Then you're blowing me off on purpose. Is it

about what happened?" He switched out the sexy timbre, now he sounded all business.

"We both need some time to think." What I didn't tell him was the 'we' in that sentence was really me. My thoughts were foggy. One minute I was sad about Max, the next I was daydreaming about Dexter.

"So what am I supposed to do? You're my assistant, remember?"

"Being your assistant and being your harlot are two very different things." My voice was tight. I tried to restrain my emotions.

He cleared his throat. "See, you're wrong. I really care for you, Crystal. I always have. You had to know that. Did you think all this stuff between us was just a coincidence?"

I wasn't sure if he expected me to reply to that last statement or not. Of course I knew. What I couldn't explain is why I let him get as far as he did with me?

I loved Max.

I took my vows serious.

I liked being married.

"Look, I've got to go." I spoke so fast, my words ran together.

"When will I see you again? When will we talk?"

"I don't know. Give me some time." I disconnected the call without giving him an opportunity to change my mind.

I dialed Max. I needed to hear his voice to erase

the feelings stirring for Dexter. Maybe hearing Max's voice would cleanse my guilt somehow. I would never tell him what I did with Dexter. Max would never be able to look at me the same again if he knew.

Max and I hadn't talked in a week. I was digging in with resentment and he was probably digging in with his self-righteousness.

"I tried to call you last night," he said, sounding about as excited to hear from me as he would have about changing one of Kia's stinky diapers.

"I'm in Delaware."

"You went home?" His incredulous tone was full of judgment, which proved how far we'd grown apart in such a short period of time. I scrolled through the still pictures in my head trying to find the moment when we took opposite paths at the fork in our lives.

"I'm spending the weekend, watching Kia." I used my how-dare-you voice. "Are you ready to come back home?"

"Does that mean you're willing to go to counseling?" He was preoccupied. I could tell by the way he snapped off the end of his sentence.

I swirled sugar into my tea, watching the white crystals dissolve. I added one more teaspoon for extra sweetness. The conversation demanded it. "I know what we need. We need you to come home most nights in time to have dinner with me. Give me at least one uninterrupted day per weekend. And stop

81

making promises you can't keep and stop sleeping around, then we'll be fine."

"And what do you need to do, Crystal? Or are you so perfect, everything and everybody needs to find a way to exist in your fairytale world?"

"You're still mad at me?"

"I'm not mad. I was never mad. I just have some standards and I insist on living by them. I won't live under your microscope. I won't spend my entire life tiptoeing around because you just might flip out by something you manufactured in your imagination."

Neither of us said anything for a long time. If I had answers, I would have put them to good use.

"Are you still there?" he asked.

"I'm here. I think we're at a stalemate." I put another packet of sugar in my tea and took a sip. It was sickly sweet.

"Crystal, I'll give you a few more days. I know what you're going through and I don't want to rush you. But you can't leave me dangling. Either you want to work on our marriage or you want to throw it away. It's your decision." He employed his courtroom voice for his closing argument.

"I'll call you back in a few days. I can't do anything from here until Walter comes back. Can you wait that long?"

"Yeah, why not." He hung up and on key, I could hear Kia on the baby monitor.

I ran upstairs to her room. The simmering wrath I

carried for my father was hard to feed when I looked into the deep brown eyes of my baby sister. She looked like the baby pictures my mother had of me. We didn't get to see each other often, but she grinned at me and raised her arms for me to pick her up.

"Hey, baby sister." I held her close.

A whole night's sleep in the same diaper meant she smelled a little sour. She needed a bath, then breakfast. The order didn't seem to matter to her a bit. She bounced in my arms like she was ready to play.

When all the necessities were done, Kia placed her head against my chest and fell asleep. I couldn't imagine my life ever being that simple. For certain, it would never be that simple again. I was carrying around a secret that was like poison leeching into my bloodstream every time I thought about Max.

I picked up my cell phone and dialed my mother. "Are you busy, today?"

"Crystal." She sounded happy to hear my voice. "I always have time for you. Are you coming to town?"

"I'm already here." I hesitated to tell her I was doing Dad a favor. "I'm watching Kia for a few days. Dad and…" I'm sure she didn't care about my father's plans. She seldom even said my father's name. It was as if she'd white-washed that part of her life off her slate. There seemed to be very little precious time for anything other than Marco for her now. But I needed to talk to her about Max.

"You know I always want to see my daughter. How about we have lunch together?"

"I'll have to bring Kia with me."

There was a long silence. She probably never expected to see my father's love child, but I couldn't leave her behind.

"Yeah, I guess that would be fine." Each word was long and drawn out like she was just learning the language.

Chapter Nine - Walter

I looked down at my wrinkled shirt and slacks.
My appearance was good enough to go find Sasha. I
entered the elevator and rode down to the lobby. The
loud music greeted me the moment the doors parted.
Vacationing in a hotel that was better known for its
spring break activity than its concierge service, I
should have expected the constant thumping.

The Black Bay Lounge was to the right of the
entrance. I expected to see her seated at the bar,
nursing some big fruity drink. The place was nearly
empty except for a few middle-aged folks that looked
as uncomfortable as I did. I made my way to the
wooden grain bar and waved to get the bartender's
attention.

"Where's the party man?" I had to talk over the
music.

"In the pool bar. Down the hall and to the left."
He had to motion with his hand for me to hear him.

I followed his directions. The music grew louder
so I had to be heading to the right location. The room
wasn't huge, but it was packed with college coeds.
The girls wore dresses so short one wrong move and
their asses would flop out. A quick glance over the
crowd revealed nothing. I walked around the
perimeter of the room where the tables were nestled. I
was just about to give up when I spotted Sasha. She
and Young Guy occupied a table with several empty

glasses parked on it. Had she been gone that long? Sasha had her eyes closed and from the way her hips rotated in the chair it was obvious Young Guy had his hand under her dress. She didn't seem to mind the lack of privacy or the fact that her partner was in the same hotel and liable to walk in. I knew that look, the moment when her face softened and all the energy seemed to drain from her limbs, the moment just before her body contracted with pleasure. From where I stood, I removed my cell phone from my pocket, zoomed in and snapped a picture just as she threw her head back and pulled his mouth to hers. I could almost see her body spasm with ecstasy.

I could only watch for a few more seconds as she devoured Young Guy's mouth. I spun around on my heels and headed out the way I came.

Rage roared through my veins, threatening to rip me open. Now there was a scar on our relationship that would never heal. I couldn't un-see the moment she let someone else into that sacred space reserved for us. I'd never be able to look at her the same again.

The mother of my daughter was now tainted. Drawing into examination so many other questions. Was this the first time for her? Who goes on vacation and hooks up with a perfect stranger? Was there a possibility that I was not Kia's father? Had I only imagined any resemblance to Crystal, hoping to see something that wasn't really there? The questions were infinite.

Outside the club, I shoved my hands into my pocket, contemplating my next move. I could have left her cheating ass right there and flown home. I could have gone back inside and snatched her away like some jealous jerk. Or I could just wait. Without a plan, I refused to be rash. Not yet. I wasn't going to leave Kia. And maybe I wouldn't leave Sasha, at least not yet. So making a scene would only make my life unbearable. The universe never seemed to stop laughing at me.

I chewed the inside of my jaw and made my way across the lobby into the casino. Maybe the bright lights and loud sounds would distract me from the rage ripping through my body. Sasha's little scene wasn't really all that surprising. The two of us had done the same thing in the beginning when we had to keep our relationship a secret.

If I'd found Tracy in the same situation, I would have melted down until someone came along to scrape me off the floor and cart me away. Sasha's behavior was almost predictable. The only thing she didn't take into consideration was whom she was playing. I was the master of manipulation. She may have just walked into my trap.

At the crap tables I unrolled five one hundred dollar bills and laid them on the table.

"Twenties," I said.

The bowman picked up the money and pushed a stack of chips in my direction. A heavyset man at the far end of the table allowed a tall willowy brunette to blow on the dice before he rolled them across the table.

"Eight. The point is eight." The stickman yelled before collecting the dice and pushing them back at the roller. I placed a neat stack of five chips on the pass line and another stack on six and four.

The roller and his woman were lucky for me. The only thing he seemed to toss was my numbers. After several throws he finally made the point. The bowman shoved another stack of chips in my direction. I held part of the roll in my fist, anything to keep my hand busy. Anger simmered in my stomach like hot tar. I couldn't get the image of Sasha out of my head. It hung there, taunting me. My mother was right, there's no fool like an old fool.

"Tonight must be your lucky night."

I looked up at dark brown eyes, skin the color of Caribbean sand, and hair as black as tar. She was trying hard to look so good, and she was successful, which had to make her a pro.

"It must be. How about you keep me company. A man can always use a sidekick." I patted the empty space next to me.

"I could be more than that." She brushed my arm with her breast.

"How about you be what I need, and right now I only need a sidekick. You got a name?" I asked before rolling the dice.

"Call me Princess." She nestled her palm on my thigh. Finally, I was getting the attention I wanted.

By the time I left the table and cashed in my chips, I had seventy-two hundred dollars lining my pocket and five bourbons eating at my stomach.

"Come up to my room." Princess's breathless request promised a night of fun. I placed my hands on the sides of her face and pushed my tongue into her mouth. The warm sweet taste was enticing enough to make me want to agree. If Sasha could have some fun, then I was certainly entitled to some, also. Without ending the kiss, Princess dropped her hand to my crotch and rubbed my hardening dick. A few years ago, I wouldn't have hesitated to romp between the sheets with a beauty like her, but at least I'd learned a few lessons. It was good to know I wasn't totally ignorant of the impact of karma.

Instead of following her round ass, I slipped her one hundred dollars and left her standing in the crowded casino.

In the room, Sasha was propped up on pillows, looking sweet and innocent. The television blared a rerun of Friends. She was naked and beautiful. There was a glow in her cheeks, but I hadn't put it there. By now I should have been numb to her charm, but she knew exactly how to suck me in.

"Where ya been? I started to come find you." She pushed her chest forward to get my attention. "I thought you were only going to watch the game." It wasn't a question. I could tell by the crinkle on her forehead she was worried.

"Is that right? You were going to come look for me buck naked." I unbuttoned my shirt and stepped out of my pants. When I was naked, I crawled into bed next to her, keeping just enough space between us.

The scent of perfumed soap mushroomed around her, along with signs of guilt. So Young Guy's finger wasn't enough. She had gone all the way. One thing I knew about Sasha, she never accepted substitutes. She was always all in. I envisioned her spreading her legs for Young Guy. His youthfulness was as alluring as my money.

"I was in the casino. I got lucky tonight and won over seven thousand dollars."

Her eyes lit up and she got up on her knees to straddle my thighs. The sexy kitten look she used to manipulate me was in place as if she expected me to hand my winnings over. "Oh wow. Let's go shopping tomorrow. I saw the perfect pair of Christian Louboutins." She sounded so innocent and young, as if a few hours of retail therapy was the only thing we needed.

"Let's do that." I pulled her towards me, just like I'd pulled Princess to me a moment ago. I kissed her with more force than I needed, but being gentle wasn't on my agenda tonight. "And what do you have for me tonight?" I reached for her right breast. She didn't push my hand away. A good sign. Maybe, my senses were off. Maybe she hadn't gone all the way with Young Guy. Maybe it was just an innocent fingering, and nothing more. And maybe I was getting feeble-minded as I grew older.

She didn't pull away when I kissed her neck or sucked her breasts. I closed my eyes. With a little effort I could pretend she was Princess and the fantasy I wanted. But when I tried to slip my finger inside of her, she grabbed my hand.

"Not tonight, honey. I'm really tired. You understand don't you? Look how late it is." She rubbed her hand along my bare chest.

There it was, the area off limits to me because she'd already worn it out tonight.

I dropped down in the bed, flat on my back. She knew what the move meant.

She winced, but I pretended not to see her discomfort. I wouldn't relent. Revenge was foreign to me but, as its ugliness devoured me, I intended to take out all my frustrations right where they began. If Young Guy could get a piece of her, than she should have offered me anything I wanted.

I was the one funding all her expensive habits.

Taking her on lavish trips.

Putting up with her tantrums.

The father of her child.

I even took her back when she severed my marriage. She owed me a debt that wouldn't easily be paid.

"Suck my dick."

Chapter Ten - Tracy

I set the phone back on the receiver and stared at it. Crystal and I talked at least once a week, but she'd never mentioned coming to Delaware and babysitting for her father. Was she trying to protect my feelings or was she hiding something? My maternal instincts told me it was the latter, since I really didn't care about Walter's life and everyone knew it. I might have even sung it from the mountaintops when I married Marco.

Was the universe trying to send me a message? Crystal was showing up with the baby. It didn't matter that it was Walter's love child, it only mattered that suddenly babies were circling my head like Valentine's cherubs. Last night I dreamed I was juggling babies while trying to slice a blueberry cobbler. When I woke up, I was almost certain I smelled the scent of talc and fresh sugared blueberries. Was it just a coincidence that Crystal was showing up today with one in tow? Was I supposed to look into those innocent baby eyes and suddenly want one of my own? True to his word, Marco hadn't mentioned starting a family again. Too bad his silence didn't alleviate my self-inflicted pummeling with thoughts of infants.

I opened the pantry door, and three packs of tuna, a half empty jar of peanut butter, and a box of frosted flakes welcomed me. None of which would make a good lunch. The large refrigerator was no better, only leftovers. I had to think of something.

Marco breezed into the kitchen and kissed the top of my head. "Why the troubled look? Was that bad news on the phone?"

"It was Crystal."

"Oh yeah. How is she?" He reached in the refrigerator and pulled out a bottle of Perrier.

"She's coming for a visit, in about an hour." I stared at my husband's flat stomach. Just when I'd gotten familiar with how handsome he was, I found something else to admire about him.

"Is Max coming with her?"

"No. She's bringing Walter's baby." My words landed like a grenade. He put the unopened bottle on the counter and came to stand in front of me.

"Say that again." He pulled me into his chest and rubbed my back.

"Yeah, you heard me. She's babysitting for Walter this weekend and she's bringing the baby here when she comes. She also gave Walter our number and he wants us to have lunch next week." I stared at Marco, willing him to say something comforting.

"By us, you don't mean you, me and him? Do you?"

"He didn't ask me to bring you along."

"Should I be worried?" His brow crinkled.

I wrapped my hands around his waist and looked

up into the prettiest hazel eyes I'd ever seen. "You've made me happier than I ever imagined I could be. My heart beats for you now. You have absolutely nothing in this world to worry about. Trust me."

He kissed me. His tongue was warm and the intensity was unmistakable. He was claiming me the same way my words claimed him.

"Are you okay with meeting him-Walter? You look like you've eaten something sour."

"I'm glad Crystal has managed to have a relationship with her father. I just wonder why she didn't mention any of this to me when we talked last week." I looked up at Marco's face. "Maybe that's the reason for Walter's call. Maybe he wants to talk to me about Crystal." I placed my head on his shoulder, trying to absorb some of his confidence.

"I think I'll run some errands. Crystal always seems to clam up when I'm around. I'll give the two of you time alone."

Marco was right. My daughter was always so formal around Marco. She hadn't gotten used to the idea of me with another man. I guess in her eyes, I would always be connected to her father.

It took months for me to stop thinking about my relationship with Marco in tentative terms. I kept thinking it was just a fling to help me get over my failed marriage. But each month we grew closer. I couldn't wait to see him, to touch him, to make love to him. It was like a schoolgirl crush. The last year seemed to skip by in such blissfulness, I was almost scared to be happy, feeling like I should have shared my joy with someone who needed it.

When I moved into Marco's condo, I'd made a few changes to the all masculine interior. Taking small steps just in case it didn't work out. It still looked more like his place than our place. When we signed the contract on the cute two story with just enough land around it to be called a single family home, I felt like I was really making progress.

In the last year, Crystal had only set foot in the condo twice. For Mother's Day and Thanksgiving. Both times she couldn't have looked more uncomfortable, as if she expected a roach to crawl into her designer purse and hatch hundreds of babies as soon as she returned home. For her to volunteer to come for a visit, with no special holiday on the calendar, set my mother radar on high alert.

The bigger question for me was how I would react to the baby that had that set the deterioration of my marriage into motion. Based on the way things had turned out, maybe I should have a gift for the little bundle of joy. If I'd ever doubted God's master plan, today was going to be a major test. One thing I'd learned in my time on earth was, God had a sense of humor, even though I didn't think he was always very funny.

Exactly an hour later, Crystal rang the doorbell. Usually she was several minutes late. At

Thanksgiving she'd arrived a full two hours behind schedule. We had just moved beyond the hors d'oeuvres and were sitting down to dinner. I'm sure it was part of her passive aggressive protest. I prayed one day she would be strong enough to be more direct with her hostility.

I wiped my palms against my white jeans and took a deep breath before opening the door. There used to be a time when being with Crystal wasn't fraught with so much emotion, but now it was a constant tightrope walk. It seemed like everything I said seeped under her skin like ancient scarabs emitting poison as they made their way to her heart.

"Hello baby." I stepped across the threshold to kiss her cheek.

She came through the door with a stroller that looked like a major piece of equipment. I didn't want to look at the baby, but I couldn't help myself.

"Hi," she said. Gone was the anxiousness I heard over the phone. There was an artificial ring of chipperness in her voice. Crystal had so many layers. Most of them I couldn't penetrate anymore. Hopefully, Max could or she'd drown under the weight. "I guess it's about time you met my sister. This is Kia."

Hearing her call the baby her sister was like a slap. I didn't want her to give Walter a pass for his indiscretion. I guess I wanted her to say half-sister or a bunch of other sordid synonyms I'd come up with.

But the minute I looked into Kia's soft round face and pink lips, I understood why Crystal adored her sister.

I kneeled in front of the stroller and looked into eyes that could have been Walter's. "Crystal, she's so precious."

"I know this must be uncomfortable for you, but I couldn't come to town and not at least pop by to see you." Crystal unbuckled Kia from the contraption like a pro. She'd done it before, that was obvious.

"Not at all. Come on back, lunch is ready. I hope you still like tuna." I waved her toward the kitchen and held my breath. "It's not fancy, but it was the best I could do on short notice. I know you used to like it."

"It sounds delicious. Did you make it with pickle relish?"

"Of course."

She hoisted the baby onto her hip. "Is Marco here?" she asked while remaining in the entry.

Only when I assured her we were alone did she follow me.

We were seated for almost an hour talking about Kia's antics and so much trivial stuff, she had to be making it up as we sat. Since Crystal got married, I didn't know the day to day activity of what was going on in her life, but I was willing to bet she hadn't just dropped by with her sister to talk teething and baby's first steps with me.

Her skin looked sallow and the sparkle was missing from her eyes. It was the same unhappiness she'd exhibited when she didn't have a date for the senior prom, and when she'd come home from her honeymoon to find her grandfather had died.

"Your father called me. He wants us to have lunch next week. He said you gave him my number. What's going on?" I positioned my chin in my palm while waiting for her to answer.

"He said he had to talk to you about some financial stuff." She shrugged. "It was okay, wasn't it?"

I busied myself pouring ice tea into both of our glasses. I wish she had asked me first, but I said, "Sure. It's not a problem." I never wanted to put Crystal in the middle of the mess between Walter and me. Next week I'd get to the bottom of what he wanted, and I knew it had nothing to do with finances. We'd resolved all that stuff before signing the final divorce papers.

"How's my son-in-law? I haven't heard from him in months. Is he still working long hours?"

Crystal grunted and took a bite from her sandwich.

"Who's taking care of him while you're down here?"

"He's a big boy. I'm sure he's managing just fine." The edge in her voice was like sandpaper on concrete.

"I see."

Talking to Crystal was like pulling thread through

a needle. If you didn't line it up just right, you weren't going to get any sewing done.

"Are you going to tell me what's really going on?" I asked when we had finished lunch and she didn't make a move to pack up the baby stuff and leave.

At first she stared across the table at me. The little girl emotions that scrolled across her face were easy to read. Her bottom lip trembled just as her eyes filled with unshed tears. "Max left me."

My heart jerked against my ribs. "What happened? When…" I stuttered, my thoughts coming faster than I could get them out. Crystal seemed determined to self-destruct and now she was too old for me to save her. Just a few years ago, she was so happy and cheerful I thought it would take more than the earth's gravitational pull to keep her feet on the ground.

"A week ago," was all she volunteered. Tears collected on her bottom lashes.

"Oh baby, I'm so sorry." I wanted to gather her in my arms and hug away the pain like I used to do when she was younger. But the look she gave me dared me to move. "Why, Crystal? Did you all have a fight? What are you going to do?" I examined her face, trying to find the carefree girl she used to be. Her father and I stole that from her and I wanted to lash out at Walter again for the destruction he'd caused.

"He was cheating, Mom. And I refused to put up with the lies and deception." Her words were hurled across the table with enough intensity to make me wince.

I clutched my chest to keep my heart in place. Crystal had a flair for exaggeration, especially, now since I'd divorced her father. But, she couldn't be embellishing this story. There was no purpose.

"Darling, are you okay? I'm so sorry," I said again. I understood her fate and the hurt she must have been feeling. I wanted to strangle sweet smiling, Max for hurting my child. "What happened? Did he tell you he was seeing someone?" I measured my response to diffuse the hostility circling us.

"I saw him with a blond. He tried to tell me she was a client, but I'm not an idiot."

I exhaled. This wasn't the ironclad explanation I was expecting. Our sins visited on our child. "Maybe he'll come to his senses. Maybe you just need to give him a little time."

"Ha." There was cruelty in her laugher.

We sat for several minutes without saying anything. Her unspoken accusations against me floated on the air between us like static. Anger consumed my once mellow daughter, and as her mother, it saddened me that I couldn't hold her hand and walk her away from its grip.

Kia smacked her chubby palms on the table and bounced up and down. For her, this was part of a game.

"Is it possible she really was a client?" I tried to remove any challenge from my voice.

She drilled me to the chair with her stare. "I saw them together. I didn't need a notary to validate what I saw." She hoisted the baby into her arms, and stood. "I better get going. It's time for Kia's nap."

"Honey, I didn't mean to question your judgement, but Max is your husband, give him the benefit of the doubt."

"Why should I?" She spoke so loud, Kia dropped her bottom lip and started to fuss.

"You're upsetting the baby. Let me take her."

Crystal shoved her sister into my arms and made her way to the bathroom. She tried to hide the tears, but I saw them.

I walked Kia over to the large window overlooking the cityscape. The view was great, but soon I'd be able to glance out and see grass again. I began to coo to get her to settle down. She pointed to a starling that strutted back and forth on the sill. A string of gibberish accompanied her excitement. As long as she wasn't crying, this was perfect.

I heard Marco's keys in the lock, and then he eased beside me. "Look at you. You're a natural." Marco kissed my cheek. "So this is the little one. She's a doll." He rubbed his hand along my back. The faraway look told me he was already imagining the two of us with one of our own.

102

A wave of cold chills rushed over me. I felt trapped and needed to diffuse the moment. "Crystal's in the bathroom. She's upset."

"What happened?"

I shook my head. The last thing I needed was for Crystal to walk out and hear us discussing her. I'm sure she'd mark it down as another betrayal. "We'll talk later." I whispered.

"Can I hold her?" Marco held out his arms with a big, wide smile. Kia leaned toward him. Pure happiness glowed in his eyes. To deny him a child would be a sin. It seemed like such a simple request from a man who asked for so little from me.

Crystal cleared her throat, interrupting the peaceful tableau. "I'd better be going." Her eyes were still red, but at least she didn't look like she was going to burst.

"Are you okay?" Marco asked her.

I held my breath and waited for her to unleash another round of hostility, directed at him this time.

"It's my marriage, Marco. I may have screwed up everything." The tears were back. Instead of running away from him like she'd just done to me, she let him lead her to the sofa. With the baby still balanced on his knee, Crystal told him the whole story. More than she'd shared with me. And he didn't have to coax one detail out of her.

Chapter Eleven - Tracy

I sat in the sterile white examination room, eyeing the stirrups. After mulling it over in my head for what seemed like years but, was only a week, I was going to do it. Just bringing up the topic of having a baby with the doctor, felt like a commitment.

Love makes you do strange things. If someone had asked me a year ago about having more children, I would have run them over with my car. Carla had an endless litany of baby trivia that would drive away the most ardent mother-to-be. But for my darling husband, the idea didn't repel me as much anymore. The thought of having a son sent my heart racing.

After raising a girl with all her fickle moods and manipulations, it would be wonderful to parent a boy. Crystal and I used to be so close, sharing everything, giggling at the silly antics of others and discussing personal disappointments. But since the divorce there was a divide between us that I couldn't seem to close.

Doctor Jefferies breezed in without looking at me. She went straight to the computer monitor across the room and began tapping the keys. "Good morning, Ms. Ferrara. How are you?" Without waiting for me to answer she continued, "Has anything changed since last year?"

I had exactly five minutes to discuss all the questions I had listed on the paper shoved in the bottom of my purse before she started pushing and poking at me. Wasting time was out. "I'd like your opinion about having another baby."

She turned and actually made eye contact with me for the first time since entering the room.

"Well, I wasn't expecting you to say that." The smile on her face was the biggest I'd ever seen on the serious doctor. She glanced back at the monitor again. "Well, I see no reason why you shouldn't. Let me finish the exam and we can talk afterwards. Hop up." She patted the table and I followed her directions.

After the hard part of the examination, I exhaled when she moved to the less stressful elements, where all I had to do was breathe in and out and let her examine my heartbeat, my lungs, and my breasts.

"Do you know many women who have babies at my age?" I stared at her, ignoring her cold fingertips on my breasts.

"Lots of women are waiting later to have children. You know, careers, following their passions, first, second marriages." Her face was serious, as if my breast was a melon she was testing for ripeness.

"My excuse is a second marriage. My husband and I have been discussing the idea." I loved calling Marco my husband. The possessiveness of the words solidified our marriage. He often referred to me as his wife and every time he said it my stomach flipped with excitement. It was a feeling I hoped never went away.

Her lips pinched and she lingered on my left

breast. I doubt she even heard my response.

She continued to knead the same spot. Why didn't she move? This part of the exam usually only took a minute. She'd been at it for three, that's more than a minute per breast. The intensity in her touch chased all my baby questions away, replacing them with a fear that pricked every inch of my skin.

She looped around and came back to the same spot. The pressure of her touch increased. I tried to focus on the speckled ceiling tiles, but I kept going back to the earnest look on her face.

"Is something wrong?"

"Do you know you have a lump in your left breast? Right here." She lifted my hand and placed my index finger on the spot she'd been studying just below my armpit. "Do you feel it?"

I was looking at her mouth, I heard the words, but they didn't register, blocked by my carefully constructed protective coating. "What did you just say?" I let her apply my finger to my breast. She had to be mistaken, but I'd pretend along with her. My life was wonderful. The only time I'd been happier was when Crystal was born. All those years when my first marriage had tormented me seemed like someone else's life. Most days I couldn't even pull up those ugly memories anymore. So Dr. Jefferies couldn't be taking that away from me. I deserved this joy.

Now.

With Marco.

With all earnestness, I tried to concentrate on the spot where she'd focused her attention.

I felt nothing.

I was a regular checker, she had to be mistaken. In an instant I turned cold. Had someone turned down the thermostat or adjusted the vent to blow only on me? I started to shiver.

I tried harder but felt absolutely nothing. "You can't be serious, can you? I mean there's no lump, right?" It wasn't until I started asking the questions that my heart kicked into a higher gear. I pushed up on the table to get a deep breath. I was suffocating.

"I don't want to alarm you." She pushed her chair away from the exam table to flip through the screens on the monitor. "Your last mammogram was…"

"I had one a few months ago." My false boldness fell flat. I couldn't conjure up a vision of the cold plates squeezing the life out of my ample breast.

"It was over two years ago." She started ticking the keyboard. No doubt recording my lack of diligence.

"Doctor, you're scaring me. Is it cancer?"

She was slow to turn around and make eye contact with me. "Don't start to worry until I tell you there's something to worry about. Here's a script. I want you to get an ultrasound and mammogram as soon as possible. I'll ask my assistant to see if she can get you an appointment today."

"It's got to happen today?"

107

She stopped writing. "Let's not wait too long. If you're free this afternoon, let's try to get it done." The way she said *let's* was supposed to make me feel better, as if we were in this private hell together. It wasn't working.

Hundreds of questions swirled in my head, but none of them made it to my mouth. I was too young to have breast cancer. Married to the real love of my life for just over a year. He deserved a whole wife, not a sick one. We were going to have a baby. My life was just beginning even though I was in my forties, the years before didn't count.

Doctor Jefferies spun around, exiting the room so fast I thought she might have been on the receiving end of the bad news.

From the edge of the exam table, I swung my legs back and forth. It was the only part of my body I felt in control of. Was the universe speaking to me again? Telling me I was crazy for entertaining motherhood for the second time.

I pulled on my clothes as quickly as I could. The sooner I got out of the confining room, the sooner I could pretend this whole afternoon was just an aberration. Before I could slip on my shoes, an assistant walked in the room with a cordless phone in her hand. After she was done, I had an appointment in two hours.

I drove to the clinic, then sat in the car, without the company of the radio, until it was time to go inside. Once I was inside and had been ushered into another examination room, I managed to strip from the waist up and lay on another examination table without asking a thousand questions.

####

I arrived home and parked next to Marco's empty garage spot. For the second time in one day I sat in a silent car. There was enough commotion going on inside of me, I didn't need the added sound of a radio.

Could this really be happening to me? I knew it wasn't a dream because my hands were cold and my heart had picked up a new rhythm that was too fast to sustain for a lifetime.

For the first time in my life, I was in love with a man who loved me back. The need to look over my shoulder all the time was finally fading. I didn't doubt myself or feel like something terrible waited around the corner for me. Only, there was something terrible waiting for me. Lurking inside my body, just bidding time to attack the moment I got carried away with my new happy life.

Every day with Marco was better than the day before. The joy wasn't waning. As hard as I tried, in my head I couldn't put together the proper collection of words to tell Marco we might be in for a paradigm shift. Our wonderful life was about to veer off course and into a ditch.

I wanted to believe I wasn't sick, and as long as I didn't say the words, then it wouldn't attach itself to me.

I opened the door and climbed out of the car. All I had to do was get from the garage through the front door of the condo. Once inside I could fall apart, or cry or wail, and not a moment sooner.

A seam in the concrete floor caught my heel. The light gray Cadillac that was always parked closest to the door helped break my fall. I snatched off the pretty shoes and threw them under the car. Two weeks ago, I would have never thought of trashing such an expensive pair of shoes, but anything that wanted to hurt me now had to be cast away.

I made it to the condo without another incident. I hadn't shed a tear or collapsed into a glass of wine. But the fat person inside of me was singing for a comfort meal and I owed it to her to give her what she needed.

By the time Marco arrived home, an extra cheesy macaroni and cheese was bubbling under the broiler in the top oven, crispy fried chicken was resting on two sheets of two-ply-paper towels and a rum cake with extra rum was in its last few minutes in the lower oven.

"Something smells good. Don't tell me you cooked tonight. I was going to take you out for dinner." Marco kissed me and wrapped me in his arms, swaying me just slightly in a gesture I'd become accustom to.

"I don't feel like going out tonight. Let's stay in."

He sniffed. "Ah, you've cooked all your favorites, which means you've had a bad day. What happened? Is something wrong? Has someone upset my short-haired princess?" He leaned back and searched my face, alarm registering in his eyes.

"Can we eat this delicious meal, first?"

"Tracy, I won't be able to eat a bit until I know you're okay. You know that." The tension in his voice crept up with each word. There was no stalling.

"Sit down, sweetheart. I have something I need to share with you."

"That doesn't sound good." Worry lines etched his face.

I wish I could have found a soothing way to share my news with him, but having it pent up inside me all day, I couldn't help but blurt out the words.

"The doctor found a lump. The ultrasound confirmed it. She wants to do a needle placement biopsy. The appointment is scheduled for next week." Saying it aloud was exhausting. I half expected to feel uplifted after getting it out. Instead, I didn't have the energy to say another thing.

"Next week. Can we get the appointment moved up? Would that make you feel better to get it over with sooner?"

"That was my first question. It's the soonest they can get me in." I never thought I could get tired by just talking, but rehearsing it for Marco took too much energy. "Suppose I have cancer? Suppose some doctor has to remove my breast? The scars are hideous and even if I get reconstruction, I'll be disfigured."

"You'll still be fabulous. Nothing is ever going to change that. Remember last year when we went skiing in Vail and I clipped that tree and tore a hole in my leg?" He paused, waiting for me to acknowledge I was listening, and rolled up his pant leg. "You held my hand while they stitched me up, helped changed the bandages, and didn't complain once when we had to sit out the remainder of our vacation. If it comes to that, I'll do the exact same thing for you. I'll even make you a toddy with extra honey." With his index finger he lifted my chin. "Now which one of these beauties is the trouble maker?"

I knew he was trying to make me smile and I loved him for the effort. "The left one."

He placed his hand over my breast and applied just enough pressure to let me know his hand was there.

"What are you doing?" I put my hand on top of his.

"I'm just sending good vibes through you. Letting that lump know our love is stronger than it is. And whatever you need from me, you know how to get my attention."

After all the turmoil that tore my day apart, I'd

managed to get by without shedding a tear. But hearing Marco's commitment without having to drop down on my knees or deliver my soul on a silver platter made tears gather in the corners of my eyes.

I caressed his chin. The roughness of his five-o-clock shadow was comforting. Words eluded me. Finally, I'd found the safety net I'd been looking for. But I couldn't help feeling like we were being cheated out of our happy ever after.

"Have you told your mother, yet?"

"No, she's probably playing bridge with her group. Besides, I don't want to get her worried unless I know something definitive."

He nodded and tightened his arms around me. "Honey, don't torture yourself. Don't spend the next week worrying about something that might not be an issue." He spoke slow and calm as if he was measuring his words. I couldn't see his face. I had enough fear for the both of us. If my strong, intelligent husband was uncertain about the outcome of the biopsy, I didn't want to see it. The least bit of doubt from him would have crippled me.

Chapter Twelve - Crystal

As long as Dad and Sasha vacationed in the Caribbean, I was happy to stay at their house and bond with my sister. I didn't foresee a lot of opportunities for us to get together until she got her driver's license and could meet me on more neutral territory.

The moment Dad and his live in girlfriend - I would call her a common-law wife, but I doubted if they would remain together long enough to meet the legal statute-returned from their trip looking a little more tanned and a lot more strained, I packed my bags and vacated the property in a total of ten minutes. Kia cried for me while Walter stood in the driveway with her in his arms. Tears streamed down her round little face as I walked to my rental car. Walter bounced her against his chest, but it didn't seem to be working.

Growing up, I never longed for a sister or brother but now that I had one, I understood all the hype. I didn't feel so alone in the world anymore.

The moment I drove away, pressure expanded in my chest like my heart was going to explode. When I was young I always had a safe haven. But now I was untethered. I didn't feel at home with my father, probably never would again. My mother had a new love, and the last thing she and Marco needed was a third wheel sitting around interrupting them. The

114

empty condo I was supposed to share with Max wasn't welcoming without him.

My cell phone rang from the passenger seat. Dexter's number flashed across the screen. Hearing his silky voice might alleviate some of the unhappiness eating at me. I wanted him to ask to see me. If Max didn't want me, someone else did.

I pulled over on a side street and answered.

"I was beginning to think you were avoiding me," Dexter said.

"Maybe I should." I looked through the windshield, focusing on nothing.

"I want to see you." His words were loaded with lust. "How about tonight?"

"I'm in Delaware."

"I'll come to you."

"How? You don't own a car." I tried to lighten the intensity of the conversation, even though my body was heating up.

"Let me worry about that. I can hire a car and be there in three hours."

"No Dexter. Give me some time. Please."

"For what, so you can forget about me?" The pitch of his voice was edging up.

"So I can think. Get my life together."

He was quiet for a long time. I could hear him breathing. "When are you coming home?"

I started to tell him a lie, to tell him next week, but I wanted to see him. The thought of pushing him away made me ache. "I'm coming back tonight."

"Then why can't I see you?"

I sighed. This conversation was making me anxious. I was married and I was doing exactly what I'd accused Max of doing. "Let's talk tomorrow."

"Fine, Crystal." The line went dead.

I should have driven straight to the Jersey Turnpike and headed home. But I didn't. My problem was where to go? I didn't want to go to my friends and let them know there was trouble in paradise already. But the idea of returning to the condo, living there alone and wondering exactly what Max was doing overwhelmed me.

My mother and I used to share everything. I was probably the only girl in my high school class who told her mother the night she gave up her virginity. I didn't keep secrets from Tracy, but it was now obvious to me she couldn't make the same claim.

I'd never had to share my mother with my father. Walter was always too busy with his life to care what we did. He seemed to be happy to have us go off and do things without him. But Marco was always there, tending to Mom's needs, smiling at her and kissing her, not leaving any room for me.

Without calling ahead, I headed towards my mother's house. It was five in the afternoon, either it was too early for her and Marco to be knee-deep in passion or they were taking a much needed break.

I pulled into the first available parking space in

116

her building's garage and dialed her number.

"I'm still in town and I wanted to see you before I head out."

"Err…okay. Where do you want to meet?" She sounded about as happy to hear from me as she would a telemarketer.

"I can be at your door in two minutes. All you have to do is buzz me up."

"Oh." That single word hung between us.

"Mom, are you okay? Are you sure you have time for me? If you and Marco are busy—"

"No, Crystal, it's not that. Come on up."

She was standing in the door when I stepped off the elevator. It wasn't the welcome I expected. She'd sounded distracted, but now there was relief in her eyes. She wrapped me in her arms. It wouldn't be the first time I misinterpreted her remarks.

She held my hand and led me to the sofa. This mother was hardly recognizable from the one I grew up with. She was much thinner now and wore her hair longer. Gone were the loose clothes, replaced by fitted pants and a clingy top. Instead of her signature scent of Dolce and Gabbana's Light Blue, she now switched up from season to season. It was almost as if she'd just found out the world could be a fun place and she wanted to experience it all. I shouldn't have been so mean to her about the divorce since she was so much happier. But I used to live in a wonderful world, where my parents revolved around me. I didn't mind sharing them with each other. It was the idea of sharing them with their new mates that caused my skin to itch.

Tracy flopped on the sofa and tucked her legs under her butt. "What's up?" Even though the words sounded chipper, her face was cast in sadness.

"Why are your eyes red? Have you been crying?" I leaned closer to her to get a better look.

She waved away my question. "You go first. What's going on, baby?"

I rubbed at a spot on my shirt, probably Kia's drool. I wanted to tell her about Dexter. I needed to tell someone, but the words wouldn't come, only shame. "I'm all alone."

"What's that now?" Her eyes were opened wide. "You and Max can work things out."

I twisted the hem of my shirt around my index finger. "My life isn't turning out quite like I thought. I envisioned graduating from college, getting married, moving to New York and being the happiest person on earth." I used my hand like I was pointing to this wonderful banner above my head. "None of those things have happened for me. I look in the mirror and I don't know the person looking back at me." I was on the verge of crying, but I pushed down the emotion.

"Oh baby." She gathered me in her arms, stroking my back much like I'd stroked Kia's to get her to sleep. "Is it about the blond you mentioned?"

I loosened her grip on me to see her face. This was the time to tell her I had feelings for another man. Strong feelings. Would she think I was like Walter? There was no doubt she still held him in contempt.

I couldn't risk it. "That's only part of it." I looked up at her, her eyes were so sad. "I don't know what sets me off, but anymore I'm always on edge. I don't trust him."

She shook her head and looked away. "My whole life I tried to keep the ugly stuff going on between me and your father away from you. I really did, and this is the reason why." She spoke softer. "Max is a wonderful guy. Give him the benefit of the doubt."

"But I'm not going to let Max hurt me like dad did you."

She took a deep breath. "Crystal, no matter what happened between your father and me, I can honestly say I had to go through that to get where I am today. There was no other way. Don't discount your marriage out of fear. Love him with as much gusto as you can and don't look back."

Now she had tears in her eyes.

"I don't want to be hurt." My voice came out high and whiny.

"True love is worth a little hurt. Believe me." She squeezed my hand.

The house was so quiet, we could have been sitting in a library. For several minutes, neither of us said a word. My thoughts whirled fast as I tried to sort through them. This was the most comfortable I'd felt with my mother in a long time.

"I have something to tell you, Crystal." She whispered the words.

"What? What is it?"

"I went to the doctor. She found a lump."

The words slammed against my heart like a fist, leaving me unable to speak. I must have looked like a scared child. I felt my bottom lip pop out and tears drip down my face.

"Are you okay? Maybe I shouldn't have told you my troubles," she said in a tone that took me back to the mother of my childhood. "You're going through enough already."

I couldn't hold back the tears. I needed to be strong, rattle off some supporting clichés I'd picked up from some sitcom I'd watched on television - everything is going to turn out okay, this is not the end of the world, a lump doesn't mean cancer. But I had nothing meaningful to say. I should have gathered her in my arms, stroked her back and let her cry on my shoulder if that's what she needed.

I couldn't speak.

I couldn't breathe.

I was frozen.

####

The condo was exactly the way I left it. If I half-expected Max to come around the corner of the bedroom and welcome me home, that didn't happen. The pair of sandals I'd decided not to take with me were still by the door.

I felt heavy, weighted down with my mother's news. I never came up with those comforting words for her. I should have paid closer attention when I was a child and she cooed around me whenever I had the sniffles.

If someone asked me about my drive back home, I would have said I was dumbfounded. How I made it from Delaware up the Turnpike, and through the Lincoln Tunnel was as mysterious to me as the lump in my mother's breast. I don't remember the two hour drive. I shouldn't have left her after hearing the news. But she was adamant that I needed go home to work on my marriage, not sitting around looking sad-faced.

I dropped my bags at the front door and flopped on the sofa. I had every intention of calling Max, but my phone rang before I made the effort. It was Dexter, again.

"Where are you now?" He sounded anxious, the same way he did when we'd talked earlier.

"In the city. Where are you?" Not that I really cared, but I was too exhausted to be original.

"In the park. I was going for a run. Why don't you come meet me at Sheep Meadow? We could talk."

"I can't. I just walked in the door. Maybe tomorrow." I lay down and stared at the ceiling. The perfectly white one that he'd painted.

"How about we meet in Chelsea later? Please don't say no. I think we need to talk about what happened."

"I don't think that's a good idea. What can we possibly say?" I closed my eyes and thought about his kiss. He was able to do to me what Max used to, before making partner and letting the law consume all of his time.

"Then let me come see you. I can be at your condo in five minutes." He talked slow now, enunciating each word as if my understanding was of vital importance. "Don't make me beg, Crystal."

"Not tonight, please." He was being too pushy. "It's late and I'm tired. Tomorrow, I promise."

He was quiet longer than he needed to be.

"That's the best I've got, Dexter. It's tomorrow or nothing." My mother's news made everything else seem less important, even my feelings for Dexter.

"Are you still my assistant? Do you plan to come back to the studio?"

"I don't know. I haven't had time to think about it. Something came up."

"You can tell me all about it tomorrow."

I ended the call and fell back against the sofa, no more connected to what was going on in my life than the cheese forming mold in the produce drawer of my refrigerator. I couldn't even pinpoint exactly when the break happened. I'd like to say Max started it with his behavior, but I had to be honest with myself. I'd

started falling apart long before Max and I were
married.

Chapter Thirteen - Walter

I sat in my office staring at the computer but paying very little attention to what was on it. Tracy was meeting me for lunch, and work-related activities couldn't compete for my attention. I ran the conversation over in my head for hours. I was ready. I just hoped she was receptive. We were good together, most of the time.

I'd checked my tie, checked the creases in my slacks, and even checked my hairline, making sure my edges were still razor sharp. My stomach rumbled with the excitement of a teenage boy on his first date. I couldn't sit behind the desk any longer. I pushed away from the desk and was in my car within ten minutes.

I sat in my car in the restaurant parking lot while I waited for Tracy to show up. I couldn't take the chance of being late, or something coming up in the office that demanded my presence.

The car radio was just loud enough to allow me to think about my trip to the Caribbean. Not that I needed to see the underbelly of my relationship with Sasha. I knew things were different between the two of us. They had been since the day Kia was born, but I didn't want it pointed out to me by Young Guy.

After my big win at the crap tables, Sasha stuck to me like toilet paper on a shoe. She found every high-end shop and managed to buy enough stuff to fill an additional bag for the trip home.

Shopping was like an aphrodisiac for her. The more she bought the easier she turned to me in bed every night. Young Guy couldn't compete with my bankroll. The disheartening part was that might be the only thing that committed her to me.

There was only one little thing that nagged at me like a rotten tooth. And I planned to rectify it today. This was more than just a lunch. This could be the beginning of something great. I still believed I was the man Tracy wanted. The one she was married to was only a stand-in for me. It might take some time to woo her, but I would. If she gave me a hint that there was another chance for us, I'd do whatever she asked since she had more reasons to hate me than I was willing to count. But if I didn't do this now, I never would.

Tracy pulled into the lot and turned the car off. I caught her profile and couldn't look away. Time had treated her kindly. She might be one year older, but she had a youthful glow that seemed to subtract the effect of the years. Just like always, her simple elegance would make any man stop and notice. The moment she stepped out of the car, the importance of our lunch made my stomach anxious.

I jumped out of the car and rushed up to her. God, she was beautiful.

"Tracy, I'm so glad you came." I made an awkward gesture to hug her, but she took a step away from me and turned my attempt into a formal handshake.

"Wow, don't you look great!" I couldn't help but gush. I'd taken extra time shaving and dressing. Picking out the shirt that went best with my complexion, the one I was always complimented on. But she didn't seem to notice my effort.

"Cut the crap, Walter. I can't imagine we have any unfinished business." She gave me a raised eyebrow.

"Let's go inside and enjoy our meal. Then we can talk. I'll get the door for you." The moment I said it, I realized that in the later years of our marriage I'd never rushed to open a door for her. That explained my predicament.

I was bumbling and fumbling like a teenage boy with a girl way out of his league. I used to sleep with this woman, why was I so nervous?

She took off for the entrance and yanked on the handle before I reached it.

We were escorted to a table in the middle of the room, which made it impossible for her to make a scene. Before sitting down, I shoved my hands in my pockets to wipe the moisture on the inside.

She spent a lot of time studying the menu and it gave me plenty of time to study her. I realized then that no matter what she said or did today, my heart belonged to her. The space that Tracy took up left no room for anyone else. That was when I realized I missed the sparkle in her eyes. When she was happy it was evident. I just hadn't made her happy often enough.

After we placed our orders she gave me her attention.

"Did you have an opportunity to interact much with Crystal while she was here?" she asked.

"I…I…well, not really. She arrived the morning we were leaving and she left as soon as we got back. We still have a strained relationship. I'm just happy she's talking to me. How about you? Do you see her much?"

She shook her head. "We talk *at* each other. But I keep trying. I think you should keep at it, too. She needs us more now than ever." She picked at her napkin while she talked.

"What aren't you saying? Is something wrong?" I touched her hand to get her to look at me. She glanced up and held my gaze for several seconds.

"If she wanted you to know, she would have told you. I won't say anything else. But we need to make sure we are showing our support for her."

"Sure. I don't understand why she is so angry with us. We tried so hard to keep all our stuff from her."

"Yeah, but it looks like what we tried to do didn't work." She pulled her hand away. "Okay, tell me what was so imperative that we had to meet today. You told Crystal you had something I needed to sign.

127

If you had papers for me, you could have sent them by courier."

"Well…" I started. I hadn't come up with the exact words, but I should have. I could tell she was growing impatient. "Are you going to give me your attention? The way you keep glancing at the door you look like you're expecting someone more important to walk through it."

"Enough chit chat, Walter. Where are the papers?" Her eyes pierced right through me.

"There are no papers. I wanted to see you. The last time we saw each other, I think you were too angry to really hear me. So I was hoping now you would be more amenable to a conversation." I paused for just a moment, gathering my thoughts. "I still miss you. I don't think I'll ever stop loving you. I hope you feel the same way, even if it's just a little. We had some good years and I think we can have that same thing again."

"Is that what this lunch is about?" She made a cruel chuckle. "You're still trying to manipulate me. All of that stuff is in my rear view mirror."

The server interrupted and placed our salads on the table. When she disappeared, I said, "I never meant to hurt you. I think we could have worked through all our problems and we could have been stronger in the end if you hadn't been so hasty."

She gave me a blank stare. "I believe all things happen for a reason. I wasn't happy and I kept trying to push that boulder up a hill. You must have been feeling the same way, but chose to deal with it differently." She pushed lettuce around her plate. "I'm happy now. Happier than I have been in years. You do know I'm married, right?" She leaned closer to me than she had all day and I caught the gleam of her huge wedding ring set.

"I know, but—"

"There are no buts. I'm married and happy. You're in a relationship and have a baby. My advice to you would be to try to make it work. Really try this time. There's not much difference between pussies, so you should try to stick with the one you have."

I settled back in my chair. "You still love me, Tracy."

"Saying it doesn't make it true, Walter. I have feelings for you. You were my first love. But what I feel for you now is something nice and mellow. You are the father of my daughter, so we will always be tied together. But the rest is history. Now let's enjoy this food, it looks delicious."

After our lunch plates were taken away, she folded her hands in her lap.

"So, can I assume the purpose for this lunch is over?" She reached for her bag. I wasn't ready for her to leave yet.

"I made a mistake. With Sasha. A big one. I know that now. Please don't make me pay for it the rest of my life." I was close to begging.

129

"Whatever is going on in your life has nothing to do with me. I resent the fact that you dragged me down here under false pretenses and thought I could or would be willing to help you. What you should be is thankful that we can be in the same room without me being totally repulsed by you. Especially after this little stunt today. Don't try so hard to be that sleazy old man. It just might come naturally for you." She stood. "What's happened to us has damaged our daughter. We need to spend our time and energy on fixing those broken pieces. Call me when you're not being selfish and you want to do something to help Crystal."

She walked out of the restaurant. All my hope departed with her, but she was right about so many things. I didn't want to be like my father, but the older I got, the more I felt like him.

Instead of going back to the office, I merged onto Route One South. Below Red Lion the traffic thinned out. I turned on the cruise control, turned off the car radio, and let the conversation with Tracy shuffle through my thoughts.

The easy ride gave me time to think, to put the pieces together so that my life made some sense. This wasn't at all what I'd envisioned my life looking like. I always imagined I would have more control of the things I did and didn't do. But what became very clear to me the closer I got to the ocean was that it was a ridiculous notion for me. I could lead in the workplace, but in my private life I was destined to follow.

The drive down Route One and back should have been plenty of time for me to accept the terms of my life. But when I pulled into the driveway of the small house I shared with Sasha, I was feeling dirty and used with no better handle on the future. So many things Tracy said about me were true. When had I slipped so far from my center? I could always count on Tracy to show me the mirror of my soul. And I could always count on her to make me hate what I saw.

She was right about Crystal. I saw the sadness in her eyes, but instead of being the father she needed, I opted for trying to be her friend. Our relationship was so shaky I didn't want to push her. I vowed to call her. No matter what antics I had to deal with first. Maybe before I could win Tracy back, I had to win Crystal back first.

I opened the car door and stepped out. Today was an opportunity for me to make some major changes and both of them burned in my stomach like hot coals.

"Sasha, I'm home." I yelled and parked my briefcase by the door. Now that she had two full-time employees, she seldom went into the bookstore, even though the sales barely cleared the expenses. Her interest in being an entrepreneur must have evaporated like her interest in everything else.

"I'll be right down." She appeared at the top of the stairs speaking in whispers, which meant Kia was asleep.

I fell on the couch and closed my eyes. Nothing about the day had turned out the way I'd hoped.

"Hey, baby," she said.

I felt her next to me before I opened my eyes. That's when I saw the shopping bags.

"You went shopping again, today." I tried to keep the edge out of my voice, but it was there. It was always there. She was a one-woman economic force, trying to keep the economic momentum moving forward.

"I drove to King of Prussia today and bought a few things. Some stuff for Kia and me. I even bought you a new tie and cufflinks." She reached for the Neiman's bags and pulled out a bundle of tissue paper.

I grabbed her hand. "Sasha, you can't spend money every day on clothes and shoes. This is ridiculous."

"We have the money. What is your problem?" She sounded like a disgruntled teenager.

"*We* don't have anything. *I* have the money and if you don't stop buying stuff from every catalog, every store, and every television shopping station, I'll cut up your cards." I dropped the unopened gift on the floor and stood. "And I mean it, Sasha."

"You wouldn't do that, would you?" She followed me into the kitchen.

I opened the refrigerator. Inside the only thing I saw was a quart of milk, a wrinkled lime, and a door full of condiments we never used.

"Yep, and I'm not talking about a month from now or a week from now. As of this moment, no more spending until I say so. Unless of course you decide to go to the grocery store and buy some food."

She pulled out the junk drawer, removed a pizza flyer, and smacked it on the counter. "If you want dinner, you better make a call, `cause I'm not cooking for you. I may not cook until the spending ban is lifted, so get used to it." She wiggled her neck and dropped her hands to her hips. Daring me to challenge her.

"What happened to you, Sasha, When did you become…this person?"

"You want to call me a bitch don't you?" She was taunting me now. I'd never seen her so angry. I should have known cutting off her favorite pastime would cause this reaction.

"If I wanted to, I would have. You're the mother of my child, but I don't really know you anymore. When did you change?"

"When you started acting more like my father and less like my lover." Her words came out with so

133

much force, I stepped back. She wanted her comment to sting and it did.

"Look, you're mad and I'm mad. Let's not say anything we'll regret."

"If I say it, I won't regret it. You're a jackass," she said through lips that barely moved.

"Really. Is that what you really want to call your meal ticket? If I were you, I'd go real easy on the name calling."

"Go to hell, Walter. You think I can't find someone else to buy me things. Have you checked out this ass lately?" She spun around, displaying her most valuable asset before grabbing the keys and marching out the door. I didn't try to stop her. She'd be back. She always came back.

Chapter Fourteen - Tracy

Sitting on the sofa watching reruns of Sex in the City was the most soothing thing I'd done since receiving the news that my health may not be as fantastic as I thought it was. If Samantha could manage to be sexy after breast cancer, then there was a possibility I could do it, too.

Trying to keep myself distracted while every minute turned into an eternity was wearing me out. Whenever Marco was at home I pretended to be upbeat and optimistic, but my insides were raw with worry. I didn't know how to turn off my fear, so it ate away at me a little every day.

The sound of the doorbell drew me away from the television and my four temporary best friends and off the recliner.

I opened the door to find Ursula. Again today her hair was in a severe ponytail, but her eyes were red and puffy. "Hey girl, what are you doing here?"

"I did it. I left Anthony." She stormed past me and flopped onto the chair I'd just vacated.

"I…I…" I'm sure my mouth was open, but I struggled to find the words.

"I'd had enough. I'm not begging for anything, least of all for love or commitment. We had a good run, but it's over." She was as nonchalant as someone ordering toppings for pizza.

"But you love him, Ursula. How can you just give

up?" I sat on the end of the sofa closest to her.

"I'm not going to let him play me. A sucker may be born every second, but I'm not one of them."

I wrung my hands for her. There was no emotion on her face, but I knew my friend well enough to know even if she wasn't showing it on the outside, didn't mean it wasn't tearing her up on the inside. I knew better than to press her on her options. She needed some time.

"Okay. As long as you're sure." I pushed off the sofa. "Can I get you something to drink?"

"No. Please sit down. I don't want you to do anything. Let's just sit here for a moment. Talk to me. Since I've been in Philly living a lie, what have I been missing in the real world? Does Carla have any new babies I need to know about?" She pushed back in the recliner to elevate her feet.

"Well, let's see. I have a lump in my left breast, and I had lunch with Walter last week. See how much you've been missing?"

I sat down. The expression on her face went from solemn to outrage.

She flipped the chair down and came to sit beside me. With my hands between both of hers she stared, without saying a word. A look of realization seemed to come over her.

"Tracy, you can't be serious. Not a lump. What are you going to do?" The pitch of each word rose with a little more alarm.

I told her the whole story, trying to leave the emotion out of my voice. She didn't need to carry my burden along with hers.

"I want to be with you." She tightened her hold on my hand. "I'm sorry I haven't been here."

"Stop it. I'm fine. Marco couldn't have been more supportive. We are trying to keep positive thoughts."

"Does Carla know?" I knew she was fishing for the pecking order. Had I told Carla and not told her? She probably thought she'd slipped from her important place in my life.

"No. I've only told Marco and Crystal. I haven't even told my mother yet. The last thing I want is for my family and friends to sit around looking sad."

"I want to be with you when you go for the biopsy. Would Marco mind?"

I assured her he wouldn't mind and the room fell silent again. The television switched to a loud commercial for maxi pads and we both stared at it like feminine protection was the most important decision we needed to make.

"You know you have to tell me why you bothered to have lunch with the pimple on the ass of earth, don't you?" she said without looking at me.

"He created a tale about having documents I needed to sign. I thought I was going to cancel, but then I thought it might be a good time to talk about Crystal."

"Well, what did he really want? To say he's sorry

again?"

"Even better. I think he wanted us to get back together." Just saying the words soured in my mouth, like I was sucking on a lemon.

"You're shitting me. Is the world full of slimy men? And why are all of them clinging to us. Aren't there other women out there they can go and harass?" Her voice rose, nearing anger.

"Excuse you. There is nothing slimy about my current husband. Thank you very much."

"Yeah, but look what you had to go through to get to him. I'd say Walter was one hell of a bull frog."

We both broke into a fit of laughter. My first since getting *the news*.

"Did you tell him about your situation?" She pointed her chin at my breast.

"No. We are long past sharing personal information with each other," I said.

"So what is up with Walter's young tart? Do you think the shine is beginning to fade already? As young as she is, it can't be that gravity has yanked anything out of place." She was almost whispering as if she thought Walter might walk in and hear us talking about him.

I laughed so hard tears peppered my eyes. "I have to admit, the idea that Walter might be just a bit unhappy made me happy. Having him crawling back to me wasn't bad either. But everything about him is in my past, and I have no intentions of going backwards.

"All I know is that he looked about the same, maybe a little thinner, a little grayer, but…but, he is still handsome. We should pray he finds his way and doesn't fall off the path again."

She gave me a fist pump. Even when she reclined against the sofa and closed her eyes, I could see the impact of Anthony etched in her face.

"I've taken a leave of absence from my job and I'm moving back to Delaware. I don't want to run into Anthony."

"Why do you care? You usually break up with them without looking back."

"He was different. I let him in. The only way to move on is to just get away." She spoke without opening her eyes.

"Where are you going to stay?"

"I checked into The Hotel before coming here. You know me. I'm still as impulsive as hell."

"Why don't you stay here with us? I can lean on you and you can lean on me."

She sat up and enclosed me in a hug. It was warm and assuring. Just what I needed to make me cry, again.

####

I eased into the warm sudsy bathtub. The water was almost too warm for comfort, but I refused to add

139

more cold water. The shocking sting of the temperature let me know I was still able to feel. For the past week, I'd been trying hard to push aside all my emotions and just hold on until the test either gave me my life back or took it all away. All I wanted to do was have a good long cry every day, but I'd promised Marco I wouldn't wallow in the unknown. Just thinking about not being able to grow old with him made my heart ache.

The lump in my breast must have been laughing at me. I had the gall to think my life was finally perfect. Nobody was entitled to perfect. Crystal and Max were ideal for each other. I'd always felt so optimistic whenever they came around. Their young love was like nothing I'd seen before. I would have wagered my investment portfolio on the two of them growing old together and living happily until death parted them. Now something had wedged them apart. Ursula and Anthony had started out with so much optimism, it wasn't impossible they couldn't overcome a few obstacles. It wasn't as if they were ill prepared for the twist and turns life was going to throw at them. I had no excuse for being so naive— thinking I'd finally gotten hold of the gold ring. I knew firsthand that life was full of tripping hazards. I just didn't expect another one so soon.

Suppose it was cancer. The aggressive kind that was not going to pause while I waited for an appointment to get the biopsy, and waited again for the technician to read the results, and then waited once more for another appointment to tell me the results. The whole time, cancer could be ravishing my body, eating away the good stuff and leaving a trail of poison behind. All the waiting was like standing on a train track while a speeding locomotive barreled its way toward me.

The knock on the door jarred me out of my sobering thoughts.

"I'm coming in." Marco said.

I looked up at him as he came through the door. Leaving him behind seemed unimaginable. I wanted to be the one to make him happy, to love him, to give him the happily ever after. I didn't want him to see me ravaged with cancer, or holding me while my hair fell out by the handfuls.

He leaned over the tub and kissed my forehead. "I'd ask you if you wanted some company in here if I didn't already know you wanted to be alone."

I cupped his face between my palms and pulled him close enough to kiss his lips.

"Are you thinking about Ursula or the lump?" The softness in his eyes matched the tenderness in his voice. At least he didn't use some cute euphemism to describe what was happening to my body. Every day he looked me in the eyes with the same amount of desire as before. I couldn't help but love this man.

"Both. And throw Crystal in the mix for extra measure." I was close to tears.

"Will you come to bed soon?"

"Only if you promise to hold me and make everything better." It was too much to ask and I knew he couldn't fulfill my request, but it felt good to have someone who cared about what I was going through. I didn't want to face this alone.

"I'll hold you and I'll always be there for you. That's what I can promise." He rested his forehead on mine. "Is that enough?"

"It's all I'll ever ask." I ran my thumb across his lips. "Get the bed warm. I'll be right there." I pressed my lips against his and fought back the tears.

He lingered a few seconds before pulling away and leaving the bathroom. The water had turned cold and not nearly as comforting. I reached for the towel, but even as I dried off, I couldn't stop shivering.

Chapter Fifteen - Crystal

I stayed in the same position, stretched out on the sofa, staring at the ceiling. My mother may have breast cancer. The words moved into a dark cozy corner in my head and began to rot. I closed my eyes and tried to imagine a life without her. Every version was sad, pathetic and lackluster. I couldn't envision a *me* without a Tracy.

She'd told me not to worry, and even though I knew she was just trying to be positive, the sadness behind her eyes told me there was plenty to worry about.

I dialed Max.

"Do you have a minute to talk?" I asked when he came on the line.

"Yeah." There was an edge in his voice that said he wasn't being truthful. He was trying to sound casual, but I detected he was in a hurry, as if he were just finishing a jog and trying to catch his breath. As always, Max had no time for me.

"What's going to happen with us? I mean…" I shrugged my shoulder even though he couldn't see me. I was flailing, if my life were a puzzle, none of the pieces would fit together. "You haven't called. Are you coming back home?" My chest ached at the sound of my own voice. It was Tracy's, pleading with Walter to love her.

"That's up to you, Crystal. I want us to go to

counseling but you've scoffed at that idea. So what happens to us is up to you."

"I want you to be honest with me. Nothing you've told me seems to be true and I can't…won't live with suspicion hanging over my head every day."

"I've always been honest. I think the only thing that would make you happy is if you could trail me every day. But I won't live like that." Through his end I heard a car horn honk so loud I had to pull the phone away from my ear.

"Where are you, now? You're not at work."

"There you go again. Good-bye, Crystal." Max had a long fuse, but I heard the irritation that was always present now.

I pressed the end button and realized I hadn't told him about my mother. This wasn't something I could keep locked up. I should have been able to discuss this with my husband. He should have given me the shoulder I needed.

I grabbed the throw pillow from the opposite end of the sofa and held it against my stomach, pressing it tight against the hurt. Rocking back and forth should have been soothing. It used to work when my mother held me in her arms to ease some unimaginable hurt. I tried to drown out the shouts that echoed my marriage was over. The bond between me and Max was severed and it looked like nothing was going to mend it together again.

My cell phone vibrated across the table. It was

Dexter again.

"Can you buzz me up?" he asked.

"Where are you? Are you downstairs?"

"Are you going to let me in or just ask me a lot of questions?"

I jumped off the sofa, fluffed my hair, hoped it wasn't matted in the back and rang the buzzer. I stood in the doorway, half in and half out so I could see him as he came up the stairs.

"Why are you here? I thought we were meeting later." I threw up my hands and went back inside with him right behind me.

He stood so close I could see the small nick on his chin, probably from his morning shave. But now there was a dark haze on the lower part of his face. Peach fuzz.

"You sounded so sad, I decided to come over." He lifted my chin. "To check on you. Is it Max?"

I shook my head. "It's my mom." I forced back the emotions. One tear would open the gates and allow everything I had pent up to rush out.

Dexter pulled me into his arms.

"Her doctor found a lump in her breast."

"Is it cancer?" There was something strong and supportive in the sound of his voice. It should have been coming from the man who was supposed to love me for better or worse. But Max bailed on the worse and I wasn't sure if I could ever forgive him for that. Of course, he didn't seem to be looking for forgiveness.

"Her biopsy is next week. This is scary. Even when Max left me, I had my anger to lean on, but this is just so, so..." A sound came from me that was more shriek than a sob. I wasn't even aware I was crying until a tear hit my arm.

"I've got a good feeling about this, Crystal. It's going to be okay." He nodded with a certainty I didn't share.

"I...I just can't imagine not having her in my life. I've been mad at her for so long. I've just taken for granted that she's always going to be there for me to dump on. I've been mean to her, blaming her and dad for all the stuff in my life that's gone wrong, and not once has she lashed out at me. Even when I purposely showed up late for her Thanksgiving dinner." Dexter let me cry and babble about my mother, my father, and my life. All the pent up stuff I needed to get out.

"Where is Max? Why isn't he here for you?" Dexter cradled me to his chest.

"Ha." The word came out high pitched and squeaky. "Are you kidding? He's at his precious job, making a good impression to the partners, hoping they'll welcome him into their prestigious circle. I talked to him a few minutes ago and he pointed out to me again, that I'm the problem. Besides, I'm not sure I even want him to come back. I'm not going to sit around pining for him. He left and my life goes on."

"Wow, you make him sound like a real jerk.

Maybe you'll be better without him. Maybe it's time—"

"Look, I don't need you examining my marriage. I've done that so much *I'm* bored with it. How about just being with me? Just for today." My throat tightened and tears filled my eyes.

I must have bawled for a full ten minutes and Dexter held me the whole time. I don't know if it was because I was grateful, or because of the tenderness he showed me, but I turned my face up to his and kissed him. He hesitated for an instant before matching my tongue. But when he did, the sensation was so intense I began to pant and claw at him like he was my salvation. By the time he carried me into the bedroom, I was burning with lust.

Dexter helped me out of my top and I unhooked his crisp khaki pants. Instead of leaving them on the floor in a heap, he held them up by the hem and lined up the seams before hanging them over the back of the chair.

"Really?" My voice dripped with sarcasm. "You're worrying about being neat at a time like this?" I waved my hand over my naked body.

"Don't act like you didn't know I was a neat freak."

"I know. I know. I'm just a little…nervous. This *is* the bed I shared with Max."

He crawled into bed on top of me, balancing on one elbow. He hovered above me for a moment before jumping back up. "I've got just the thing you need." He reached for his pants and removed two joints before crawling back in the bed.

"Are you serious? You think smoking a doobie will make everything better?" I rolled my eyes. "We don't live in Colorado, that stuff is illegal."

"Don't tell me you've never smoked a joint before?" His incredulous look dared me to be practical. "You've got to stop being uptight. Life is supposed to be fun. When was the last time you let go and really laughed? From here." He jabbed his finger at my stomach.

Even though Dexter was joking, I didn't want another man telling me I wasn't fun. I used to be the girl everybody wanted to be around, not the one they fled from.

"Oh, I'll show you, fire that baby up and hand it here." I knelt on the bed in front of him.

He twisted the end before lighting it, took a long drag and then handed it to me.

"Have you even smoked before?" he asked.

"Oh, shut up. Of course I have, but not since college. I'm an adult now." I pinched the joint between my thumb and index finger and took a pull as long and deep as Dexter's. My chest felt tight and I started coughing. Dexter took the doobie from me.

"Take it easy, slugger. You don't have to prove anything to me."

I straddled his thighs and allowed him to blow

smoke in my mouth. With each drag, the burden sitting on my shoulders grew less significant. By the time we finished the second joint, I couldn't stop giggling.

"Look at you. You're grinning like a Cheshire cat." He spoke slower than usual.

"I think you're feeling pretty good yourself," I giggled.

Dexter held the roach to his mouth and took the final drag. He shared it with me before dropping it onto the glass coaster on the nightstand.

"See, I told you all you needed to do was loosen up." He held my breasts in his palms. "You look more relaxed already."

"That's because I'm high."

"And I won't even charge you for that high quality weed from my special stash. See, I'm good for you and I'm here, unlike someone else we won't mention." His eyes were glassy and intense. There was warmth in them that tugged at the missing piece of my life.

I rolled my tongue across the inside of my cheek, not really searching for a reply. I never thought of Dexter and me and the future. Since Max had left, I seldom thought beyond the end of the day.

What was the purpose? I had no idea what was going to happen tomorrow. Whenever my thoughts drifted to the future, I backed them up and quashed the fanciful thinking.

149

Nothing ever turned out the way I imagined. In high school, when I didn't get accepted at Virginia Tech, my counselor told me I needed to adjust my expectations. It sounded easy enough, but I stayed in the dumps for weeks until I received the acceptance letter from the University of Maryland. That's all I needed to do this time. Max was gone and it was time to accept it and adjust to the new normal.

Dexter was my friend. As long as he was my friend, I didn't have to manage the relationship or think about what was going to happen next for us.

"Make love to me. We can talk later." I reached for his swollen penis and the inquisitive light in his eyes melted into lust.

By the time Dexter and I left the condo it was early evening and we were still giddy. All the overwhelming stuff with my mother and Max had taken a rest and I was having fun. I was determined to enjoy the light moments for the few hours that it would last. As soon as the effects of the pot wore off, I would probably be dropped into a vat of hot oil for sleeping with Dex again and enjoying it so much.

I was actually happy for the first time in weeks. Dexter had pulled me out of my shell and I could feel the sun on my face. The weather was warm and the promise of summer loomed just around the corner. I

GOING BACKWARDS

used to imagine Max and me exploring the city together and finding a small restaurant where we could have dinner at least once a week and be considered regulars. Nothing had turned out the way I envisioned. I certainly never thought that just months after our first anniversary we would be separated. Every time I focused on that thought, my heart sped up. This couldn't be happening to me.

Dexter was the only person excited to see me. There was a dead hole in the center of my heart, a gaping wound that must mirror every other child from a dysfunctional family. From day to day it was as if buzzards were picking at the pieces of normality I was trying so hard to hold on to. But whenever I was with Dexter, all the bad stuff seemed to slow it's descent on me.

We caught a cab and the driver let us off just short of 23rd Street. The heels I wore didn't let me walk fast, so we ended up strolling along like any couple in an intimate relationship. He even slipped his hand in mine. The feeling was comforting and I didn't pull away. We'd already shared a joint and each other, to hold hands only seemed fitting.

We made our way down 11th Street and turned onto 10th Street. The day was lovely, not too hot. I should have been walking with Max. Instead, I tried to erase any thoughts of him. Nothing good could come from being with Dexter, but I was content, and it was so much easier to ignore the warning bells sounding in my head.

Any hesitation I had vanished. For one night, just this one, I planned to have a good time. Dexter was my friend, and even though we had sex, I wasn't foolish enough to think it meant anything. There was nothing wrong with us spending the evening together.

Dexter put his arm around me and kissed my cheek.

"I thought you were going to change your mind about meeting me. I was starting to worry." He looked down at my face. "That's another reason I decided to stop by your place. Was I right?"

"I…" I hesitated. "We're here now. Let's enjoy the day, okay?" I nudged him to break the stare. He was making me nervous.

Even though I welcomed his touch, I stepped out of it. I was fooling myself, strolling through the High Line like we were a couple. I was a married woman and even if my marriage was drawing its last breath it wasn't over yet.

"Okay, it's going to be like that, huh?" Dexter sounded piqued.

We took the stairs and walked in silence, weaving through the crowd.

"So are you coming back to my studio? I still need an assistant and I think you would be great."

"Err…maybe the two of us working together wasn't a good idea."

He stopped in front of a row of sunbathers. "How

about if I promise to keep my hands to myself during the work day?"

I grabbed his hand. "You might be blocking someone's tanning rays. Let's keep moving. We can talk about it later."

He stopped again and turned me around to face him. His hands gripped my upper arms and his face was so close I thought he was going to kiss me. "I've never made a secret about my feelings for you. Didn't you notice my studio was the same color as your bedroom? That wasn't done by chance, Crystal. I'm in love with you. And you obviously have some feelings for me. Any blind person can see what's going on between the two of us. Why are you ignoring it?"

"I can't see it because I'm married."

"You're married because a piece of paper says you are. You forget I'm your jogging buddy, when you're winded you tell the truth. And the truth is, you aren't happy. I haven't seen that happy-go-lucky woman who asked me to paint her new condo in months." He tried to whisper, but I could hear him clearly, everyone around us could.

I shook my head. "Dexter…it's not that simple."

"It is that simple, Crystal." He pulled me closer. "Stop making it more complicated than it needs to be." He crushed his lips against mine. I parted my lips to accept him. His hungry tongue matched my need and even though my head warned me to pull away, I didn't. Instead, I pushed aside everything, my morals and my marriage and stayed in the moment where there were no rules or ultimatums and or heavy-handed regrets. I felt like the person I used to be. The carefree and fun one who didn't have to look over her shoulders to see if life was snipping at her heels. The person that Max had turned me into.

"Crystal." My name was yelled by a voice I knew well.

I pulled away from Dexter to find Max standing behind me.

Chapter Sixteen - Walter

I settled into the lounger in the cozy living room. Cozy, because it was so small. If it wasn't for the highball filled with whiskey clenched in my hand, I might have put my fist through the nearest wall.

When I arrived home, instead of finding dinner on the table, the baby in bed, and soft music playing, I walked in on a babysitter screwing her boyfriend on my sofa, the baby half asleep in her high chair, and Sasha nowhere in sight.

Thankfully, my fourth drink helped mellow out the irritation that simmered in my belly. I wanted it to be just the right temperature for when Sasha walked through the door. We were beyond discussion, it was time for action.

I heard her key in the lock and got to my feet.

Sasha bounced in the house, still humming some club song under her breath. She closed the door and looked startled when she turned to see me. "You're home already. I thought Thursdays were your late night," she said without meeting my eyes. "Is Kia asleep already?"

She tried to rush past me, so I grabbed her arm and squeezed it tight.

"I didn't know you were going out tonight." For now I kept the anger out of my voice.

"Yeah, well I told you some stuff was going to be different. You don't like it so well when you can't control me do you?" She tried to loosen my grip but we were a long way from finished with this conversation.

"I'm not interested in controlling you. Do you know what I found when I came home?"

"Can you tell me tomorrow? I'm exhausted." She kicked off a new pair of heels.

"Your sitter was having sex with her boyfriend on our sofa just a few feet away from Kia, who was in a soiled diaper and asleep with her dinner crusted on her face and bib."

"So the new sitter didn't work out. I won't hire her again." Her response was so sweet I thought we had changed the subject.

"Where did you find her, Sasha? Did you just grab the first person you saw walking down the street?"

"Her name was on the bulletin board at the university. I checked the references she gave me."

"And what was so important you had to switch sitters?"

That's when I noticed her attire. She wore a fire red tight-fitting dress. It was simple but very sexy. Her bare legs looked freshly waxed and glowed like new copper pennies.

"I was out with my friends."

I leaned close to her and sniffed.

She pushed me away. "What are you doing?"

"Male friends or female friends?"

"My girlfriends. And why are you grilling me and smelling me? Have you lost your mind?"

"Well, whoever the sitter was, don't hire her again. I don't trust her with my baby."

"Your baby?"

We glared at each other for several seconds. Her simple statement was loaded. She was feeding a doubt that continued to grow in me. Was there a possibility that Kia wasn't my child? That question was always lurking in my head just looking to pick up traction. If Sasha began to feed the beast, a hell would break loose in this house that nothing and no one would be able to contain.

I tried to decipher her comment. Was she trying to admit something or being vindictive? This wasn't the time to push her. If she told me Kia wasn't mine, it would rip my heart open. I needed to find out, but in my own time.

I took a deep breath. "Can we agree the next time you need to go gallivanting with your friends to let me know? I'll make sure I'm here for Kia."

"Sure, I think that's a good compromise." She kissed my cheek. "I like it when you're reasonable."

"Where did you get the shoes?"

Guilt washed over her face. "Those are old or at least I've had them for a while." She picked up the shiny red heels, dangling them from her fingers. "I'm exhausted, can we go to bed now?"

I turned off the lights and followed her upstairs.

"Is this how it's going to be between us? Always arguing or disagreeing over everything?" With her ass at eye level I couldn't help but touch her firm butt.

"You're cranky as hell. You know, sometimes I think you want to be back with Tracy."

I couldn't reply. I couldn't be that easy to read, could I? But she was absolutely right. If given another chance, I would place Tracy on the pedestal where she belonged and worship at her feet every night. It was the mistake that just kept on giving.

Sasha stepped out of her dress, and of course she wasn't wearing panties. I think she had an aversion to that particular piece of clothing. I used to think it was delightful, but now everything she did raised my suspicion.

I dropped my sweatpants and crawled into bed beside her.

"You didn't answer my question." She rested her head on my chest.

"What question?"

"Do you wish you had stayed with Tracy?"

I steeled myself before answering. I needed to deliver a convincing answer, even if it meant denying what I wanted more than anything else. But I couldn't find the words to deny my heart. "Why do you think that? It's been over a year, have I given you reason to think I'm not where I want to be?"

"Because you didn't pick me." There was panic in her voice. I thought she was on the verge of tears. A thread of insecurity ran through Sasha, buried below her surface. Whenever it poked through her shield it usually cost me dearly.

"If I hadn't confronted Tracy, I think you would still be with her. That's the mistake I made. I should have been patient and waited to see how long it would have taken you to leave her. Then I wouldn't always be wondering or looking for clues. It's driving me crazy." She took a large gulp of air. This confession must have been building up. It was as if she couldn't contain it any longer. She clung to me and cried like she was finally letting go of a burden she couldn't carry any more.

"Sasha, cut the tears. You're only raising this question now because I've challenged you about where you've been tonight."

"That's not true. I'm saying this because it's what I feel. We don't even talk about getting married anymore. You're content to be my live-in-lover."

"I'm where I want to be. I think the three of us can be very happy if we stop picking at every single thing." I was so convincing, I almost believed myself.

"Do you love me? I mean really love me like you did Tracy?" She sounded needy.

"Of course I do."

I reached for my cell phone and found the incriminating picture of her. "Since we're examining behavior, let's talk about this." I shoved the phone in her face. It took her a moment to react.

"What? What is it?"

"It's exactly what you think it is. I saw your episode in the Bahamas. I know you and Young Guy were having a really good time in the lounge and I'm more than certain that this little episode was only the beginning." There was no anger in my voice.

"I...I—"

"Don't lie to me. I'll put up with a lot of your bullshit, but I won't put up with lying." I was surprised at how quickly my calmness switched to anger. I could almost envision her and Young Guy screwing and laughing at me the whole time. "Don't try to deny it. I saw the two of you. You didn't seem to care who saw you."

"Were you spying on me?"

"I was looking for you, so don't try to flip this back on me." I almost growled.

"It was a mistake. I was just so mad at you. It didn't mean anything." She climbed on top of me, straddling my legs. She cupped my face in her hands and planted kisses on my lips and cheeks. "I mean it, baby. I love you. I always have. You know that."

I turned my face away. "I'm not sure what I know." I held her hands and looked in her face. "Have there been others?"

"Of course not. That night I had too much to drink and you were more interested in your ball game than having fun. It was one night. Only one night. Let me make it up to you." She kissed my neck and down my stomach. She reached my penis and rolled her tongue around the tip before taking it into her mouth. My anger was replaced with a heated lust that wanted satisfaction. I closed my eyes and let her pleasure me. I'd been faithful to her. Something I couldn't manage for my wife, and I had loved Tracy.

When I couldn't hold back my desire any longer, I stopped Sasha and pulled her up to me. I kissed her hard on the lips. My body was stoked for her.

I flipped her off of me and stood up. "Get on the edge of the bed." I demanded.

She crawled to the edge on her hands and knees, backing toward me. Her plump ass was exactly where I wanted it. I entered her warm, wet core. For a moment I didn't move. She hated making love this way. But I didn't care. I felt like she owed me and I intended to enjoy this moment for as long as I could. I only believed half of her story, but I knew how to make lemonade from lemons.

She contracted her muscles around my shaft and I held her hips in a firm grip and moved her back and forth, slowly increasing the pace. We were opposites, but when it came to sex, we both put up with a lot and took out our aggressions with our bodies.

"Oh, baby, that feels so good." She could have been lying, but I didn't care.

"Better than Young Guy?" I asked and slammed into her.

"Yes. So much better. I'll never stray again."

"I don't believe you." I slammed into her again. She probably thought this was a sex game. Her moans of pleasure grew louder each time I pulled out and re-entered.

She glanced over her shoulder at me. "I promise. I'll never do that again, baby."

"Cum with me." I managed to croak.

"Yes. Now."

I pushed as deep as I could into her and let it all go.

From the moment I woke up, then drove to the doctor's office, and finally settled into the waiting room, one thought consumed me. A collection of selfish decisions should have taught me so much more about life by now. But like my mother said, a hard head made for a soft ass.

As much as I wanted to believe Sasha, I wouldn't let her play me. Not again. Showing up at Tracy's job and severing my marriage was her one grand error I could never forgive her for. But the thought of her and Young Guy was just as detrimental. If her severe offenses kept mounting, she'd back me into a corner that I'd have to fight out of.

I adjusted Kia from one knee to the other. She was so consumed with her white bunny rabbit she didn't seem to mind sitting in a doctor's office.

"Walter Baptiste." The nurse called my name to escort me behind the door that was going to change my life. She led us to a small room.

"She is adorable. What's her name?" The nurse bent down to talk to Kia.

Without releasing her bunny, Kia stood behind my leg. I was her protector, but the feeling that I was about to betray her wouldn't stop nagging at me. "This is Kia." I said and picked her up.

"The doctor will be with you in a few moments." She closed the door before I could reply.

This move could change my whole life. Either it was going to turn out fine or rip my world apart. A world that couldn't stand much more turbulence.

There was time to turnaround, go back to my office and pretend I could continue on my current path. But since my divorce I'd tried to be more responsible, more realistic, and more prudent. Knowing was always better than not knowing.

The doctor walked into the room. "Good morning, Walter." He sat on a small round stool. "So I take it you've given this some thought, and since you're here this morning, I assume you want to go through with it."

I exhaled. "I've got to do this. I want the paternity test." My stomach churned with anguish, but I managed to say the words with authority, like a man in control of his destiny. "The sooner I get the answers, the better I can plan for my future." I

163

ignored the sound of blood pounding in my ears.

"Will it change the way you feel about this pretty little girl?"

"I don't know." I answered, measuring out my words. "But not knowing is eating me up."

"Okay, this will only take a minute." He opened a drawer and removed two plastic bags. "Let me do you first so the baby can see it doesn't hurt."

The feel of the cotton swab against my cheek was a reality check, but I couldn't turn back. If I planned to look in the mirror ever again, I had to follow through.

Kia cried the moment the doctor got near her, but he managed to get the sample.

"How long does it take for the results to come back?"

"It only takes two days. Do you want me to mail them to you?"

"No, I want to come back in. Just in case I have any questions." I stood with the baby planted on my hip.

He nodded.

"One more thing doctor," I said. "I want a vasectomy. Can you do it or recommend someone?" My voice didn't waver one bit.

He folded his arms and leaned against the cabinet. "Have you given this much thought? I usually like to counsel people before they take the steps of permanent sterilization."

I tightened my hold on my baby daughter. From the moment Kia was born, she'd held my heart in the palm of her pudgy little hand. But if I could turn the hourglass of my life upside down to the first time I slept with Sasha, that was the point when I'd needed counseling. That was the time for a professional to tell me to keep my dick in my pants.

"How soon can I get an appointment?"

Chapter Seventeen - Crystal

I looked into Max's eyes and held my breath. A fury blazed there like nothing I'd ever seen before. He seemed to swell up three times his normal size, bouncing from one foot to the next as if he had excess energy he needed to disperse.

Dexter widened his stance, looking like a big cat preparing for an attack.

I stood motionless between the two of them, taking it all in. If I stood still long enough without making any sudden moves, maybe no one would pounce. Visitors cut a wide path around the three of us.

Dexter kept his hand around my waist, as if I was some prize and he intended to hold on to me. I glanced back at him to see determination in the set of his jaw.

I put a little space between Dexter and me, but it wasn't big enough to give anyone the illusion of innocence.

"You know what, Crystal?" Max took a step towards me and pointed his index finger at my nose. He huffed so loud he sounded like a bull preparing to charge. "You are a piece of work. All those accusations about me having an affair." He bit down on his lip. I waited to see blood.

He held up his index finger, halting all conversation. I watched him inhale and exhale with effort the whole time I held my breath.

I wanted to say something that sounded tough to make him think I was unfazed by his presence. But whatever I was running from had caught up to me. I opened my mouth to say something that would explain away what he saw, but my throat clogged with tears. I reached for his hand, but he jerked it away.

"You know what?" he repeated, before looking up at the sky as if he was searching the universe for the right words. "I can't make a scene here. I'm going to be the responsible one, because one of us has to be. I'm going to text you the name and address of a therapist. If you're not there for the first visit, on time, I'm filing for divorce." He stopped for a moment. "I mean it Crystal. You decide."

Before I could form a single word, he wheeled around and vanished into the throng of people who had no idea my life was falling apart.

Dexter grabbed my hand. We walked in the opposite direction to the nearest stairs. My brain reeled so fast I was numb. The lack of pain was probably the only thing that made my feet work as Dexter led me off the High Line.

We walked into a small dark bar. Without the bright sunlight shining on my shame I found my tongue. "I can't believe that just happened. How did he know where to find me? Was he following me?" I wasn't really talking to Dexter, I was just talking.

167

"Crystal, I'm not that kind of guy. If you and Max are still working on your marriage, then I don't want to get in the way." He flagged down a passing server and ordered two beers.

I rubbed my earlobe. What could I say? Like Max, I was ignoring our marriage. "I have no idea what's going to happen to me and Max. Maybe my grandmother was right. I was too young to get married. I should have let Max do his grown up thing for a while and I should have done mine."

Dexter reached for my hand. "If you don't know yet, let me just put it out there. I understand if you feel like you need to save your marriage, but…" He looked towards the door and clenched his jaw.

"What? Say it." I shook his hand, trying to loosen his words.

"Okay," he paused. "I think the two of us could have something really nice. We have so much in common. I get you and you get me. We have fun together. To me, you'd never be an afterthought. Something I had to come to at the end of the day." He exhaled like he was getting something major off his chest.

"Shouldn't I try to save my marriage?" I didn't expect him to answer that question. Only I could, and I should have had a definitive reply. Most women would want to save their marriage. Tracy had wanted to.

I was wrought with so much resentment, I didn't

know how I felt. Max had walked out on me weeks ago. Now here he was laying out the demand I see a therapist or else, as if he had some special right to dictate my actions. I was used up with no reserve to draw from, because if this was my fork in the road, I was more inclined to take a seat and watch what unfolded.

"You shouldn't have to save your marriage. If Max cared about it…about you, he never would have walked out. Throwing ultimatums hardly seems the way to go."

I nodded. "But you're biased."

"I am. And, I'm being honest, also." He held my gaze. "Will you tell him about us? All of it?"

I bit my lip and looked away. My body still tingled from the way he'd touched me earlier. Dexter wasn't a fantasy anymore, he was the living, breathing, man in my life. His presence was big and he focused so much energy on me it made my heart thunder against my ribs. Max was sturdy and predictable. We made love in the bedroom, with the lights dimmed and the television on. Comparing Max to Dexter put Max at an unfair disadvantage.

"Max would never be able to forgive me, if he knew how far we went." My voice had a distant quality. I tried to visualize a future where Max and I were happy again. I might have wanted it, but I couldn't imagine it. "I don't know what I'll do. Just because he demanded I show up for counseling doesn't mean I will."

"Can you forgive his infidelity?" It sounded like an indictment more than a question.

"I don't know. I don't know if I want to. My mother forgave my father once and in the end he only did it again. And the second time was far worse than the first. Tracy has no idea I knew all about that, she would be surprised at how much I really know."

He reached for my hand and squeezed it. "Promise me you'll think about it. Don't take the traditional route and forget about yourself in the process."

"You don't want me and Max to get back together, do you?"

He positioned his chin in the palm of his hand. "I've been very open. You know exactly where I stand. I'm hiding nothing." He threw his arms wide, almost hitting the passing server.

"If Max and I get divorced I might not stay in New York. Living here was his dream. Without him I'll be free to follow my own dreams." The thought that I could move away from the little condo and the unhappiness in it made my heart speed up. I couldn't tell if that was good or bad, but at least it was something.

####

I stood in the middle of the condo and I would

have sworn I heard the whisper of my empty life, nagging at me for the mess Max and I had made. Either it was the lack of occupants or the lack of emotion, but for certain something was nonexistent in me and the place, that I was supposed to call home.

Calling my mother was out of the question. She had enough to handle right now. Next to what she was going through, this was insignificant. She was dealing with life or death issues.

I picked up the phone and dialed Ursula. My single godmother just might understand what I was going through.

"Hello there," she said when she picked up. She sounded much perkier than she did the last time we talked.

"You sound good, I take it that everything is fine with you." I was fishing for details, hoping she'd tell me what was going on with her and Anthony.

"Let's just say, I finally took the hint. I'm moving on. I've left Anthony," she said.

"I liked him. I'm sorry to hear that."

"Don't be. I think it was best for both of us." She sounded so certain. It was just like Ursula to set her mind on something and not question her decision. I could use more of her in my life.

"Have you talked to Mom, lately? I need to talk to someone but—"

"I'm staying with her until I find a new place."

"Did she tell you about—?"

171

"Yeah. I know."

"How is she really?"

Ursula took a deep breath. "It's hard to tell. She's quieter than usual. I can tell she's scared, but who can blame her? I've been giving her as much space as she needs."

For a moment, neither of us spoke. If my mother's lump was causing us both to hesitate, I couldn't imagine how she was handling it.

"I'm glad you're there for her." My voice quivered. I couldn't put it off any longer. I was about to burst from the anxiety. "Ursula, I need to talk to someone. I've done a horrible thing and I just don't know how to fix it, or if I want to."

"Do I need to know what the horrible thing is?"

I exhaled long and slow. "I'd rather not say right now. But Max has set up an appointment for counseling and I'm debating if I should go."

She was quiet for a long time. "What do you have to lose by going to a session? After a few meetings maybe everything will be clearer and deciding the future of your marriage will be easier. Go."

"You make it sound so easy," I said.

"Crystal, it really is that easy. Take it from me. Don't spend a lot of time in limbo. You can't make a future if you're wallowing in indecision.

I felt like a little girl on her way to kindergarten. "Yeah, okay." I nodded.

"And, one day soon, I want to hear what the

horrible thing is that you did."

"I figured you would. I'll be coming down in a few weeks. We'll have to talk."

"No, not in a few weeks. Call me in a few days." Ursula's firm tone left no room for discussion. I should have known I wasn't going to be able to fool her. I never could.

"Okay. I will." I almost whispered the words. I couldn't imagine telling anyone about Dexter. I wasn't sure I understood my behavior, so I was certain no one else would.

Chapter Eighteen - Tracy

Why did all the bad stuff happen to the left side of my body? My plantar fasciitis in my left foot always flared up when I decided to be a weekend athlete and run five miles through White Clay Creek Park. When my left thumb went wonky for absolutely no reason at all, my doctor called it trigger thumb. Which sounded like a cute name until it refused to get better after two cortisone shots, and required surgery. Now my left breast needed to make a starring performance and decided to harbor a lump that could change the direction of my life.

I stared at my image in the full-length mirror on the bathroom door. Behind the black yoga pants and oversized sweatshirt I was as normal as I was two weeks ago. But after today, everything about my life could be turned upside down. There was something about this moment that I wanted to remember. Maybe this was the last carefree moment of my life.

"Tracy, if you don't hurry, we're going to be late." Marco called from the entrance of the bedroom.

"I'm coming." I took one final look at myself before grabbing my purse and making my way out of the bedroom. Marco and Ursula were seated at the kitchen island. The expressions on their faces said all the things we promised we wouldn't feel. They were worried. And so was I.

Ursula jumped up. "We've gotta go."

174

"What's your hurry?" I asked as I followed her out the door.

Marco threw his arm around me and kissed the top of my head. "Tracy, it's going to be fine. I know it is."

"If you're so sure then why is your eye twitching? You only do that when you're nervous."

"That's not true. I also do it when I'm extremely confident." He flashed the dynamic smile I loved, it almost made me believe him.

"Since when?" I turned to face him.

"Ever since you got that lump in your breast." He squeezed my butt cheek. "Now let's get going."

Ursula stood at the front door with her purse on her shoulder. I wanted to do this alone, but Ursula needed the distraction. She'd been hovering around me since she moved in. Anybody who knew her knew she was the kind of person who wanted to play nursemaid. Helping me through the hardest thing I ever had to do must have allowed her to forget she had her own difficult decisions to face.

"It's about time. I thought Marco and I were going to have to carry you out of the house." Her tone was full of edge, but in her eyes was a softness that only a few people ever got to see. For just a moment, she'd dropped her shield and exposed her tender side, the one full of compassion. Before I went all mushy with tears she opened the front door and waved us in front of her.

175

"Is she always this bossy?" Marco asked me.

"Always." Ursula responded.

If the two of them were trying to distract me, it wasn't working. But I loved them for at least trying to make the effort.

By the time we settled in the Surgi-Center, my gloom had settled onto the three of us like a heavy blanket of wet sand. Marco and Ursula flipped through pages of year old magazines, and I stared at the little television jammed in the corner of the ceiling. But I couldn't hear a word and I refused to read the closed-captions.

A nurse hurried toward me with a clipboard in her hands. "Ms. Tracy Ferrara, I'm Susan your case worker for today. I'm ready to take you back. Once we get you prepped, I'll bring your husband back for a few minutes before the procedure."

I nodded because I couldn't think of anything to say.

"It's going to be okay." Marco placed his hand on my shoulders and pulled me into his arms. He kissed me like he had at our wedding as if he were trying to convey a message to me with his body. Ever since I'd told him about the appointment, it was the only time he faltered.

I followed the nurse through double doors into an open area full of smiling faced nurses in various activities. They all wore giant grins as if we were in the happiest place on earth. Hadn't they heard that anyone behind these walls was a long way from being happy? Maybe it was all a farce to make us feel better. To keep our spirits up before some doctor came along and gave us the bad news.

On the other side—the recovery side, there was probably a whole score of nurses with more moderate dispositions that were more suited for anyone who had already gotten bad news and didn't want to be reminded that others were still jovial.

My caseworker led me to a small cubicle. She snatched back the curtain as if it was some kind of great reveal, but it was only a metal chair and an examination table, hardly anything to get excited about.

"You'll need to strip down, take everything off but your panties. Put on this robe, make sure the opening is in the front." She handed me a folded gown that was as soft as a cotton ball. I was actually looking forward to putting it on. "Do you have any questions?"

"How long will the biopsy take?" My voice came out in a whisper.

"It should only take about an hour." She was half outside the curtain, talking to me over her shoulder. I must have been keeping her from something or someone more important.

Usually, when left alone by a doctor to prepare for an exam, I hurried out of my clothes and into the gown, but today I hopped up on the table and swung

177

my feet back and forth to a soothing tune playing in my head. There was no reason to be expedient. Hanging out in the world I knew was better than rushing forward into the unknown. I was the same way when I went into labor with Crystal. Instead of running to the hospital with the first contraction, I sat in the center of our bed panting. The moment she was born our lives would change, we would change, and I wanted to hold on to the present for as long as I could.

"Ms. Ferrara, are you ready?" The artificial sweetener in Susan's voice was cloying. How could she have that job and manage to sound happy? At the end of the day, did she go home and cry real tears like so many of her cases?

"Almost," I jumped down and pulled my shirt over my head. "Give me another minute please." I felt like a child caught sneaking out of the naughty chair.

A few minutes later Susan pushed the curtain aside and walked in with a clean-shaven man pushing some huge medical apparatus. "We're going to get you prepped now.

By the time the two of them finished prodding and poking me, I had to hold my left arm away from my body. The largest needle I'd ever seen had been placed into my breast. According to my caseworker and the technician it would be used during the procedure to inject dye into the tissue. That's all I could remember. The rest of their explanation sounded like gibberish.

"Aw, honey, what's wrong?" With my eyes closed, I didn't see Marco walk in, but the sound of his voice was like a snap, bringing me back from unhappy land. "Are you in pain?"

"I'm scared, Marco. I don't think I've ever been more afraid of anything. I was happy before I went to the doctor. Can I just go back to where I was? Before all this stuff…started to happen." I used my right hand to point to the needle sticking out of the side of my left breast. "This needle is so long it could jab some other vital organ."

He leaned down to me, pressing his cheek against mine. "You've got to be strong, baby. For me." I could hear the quiver in his voice that always came out when he was close to being emotional. "I've waited too long to be with you, so don't give up on us. No matter how this turns out, we will always be happy. You have my word on it."

He kissed my cheek, then my neck, and then my soul, and I believed him.

Chapter Nineteen - Walter

All I wanted to do was go inside the house, put my feet up, and have a cold beer. But my gut told me that wasn't going to happen. After being away for one week, Sasha was probably going to talk to me all night long.

I put my key in the door and walked in. Instead of hearing the television blaring, I heard smooth jazz.

Sasha charged out of the kitchen and into my arms. "Finally, you're home. I hope you're hungry." Dressed in a sheer black nightie, she pressed her lips to mine before pushing her tongue into my mouth. I felt like Santa Claus.

"Wow, I wasn't expecting such a warm welcome. Does this mean you're not still mad that I've cut your spending?" I held her at arm's length and admired her exposed flesh. "So what brought all this on?"

She hunched her shoulders. "No reason. And no, I'm not still upset about the money thing. I just wanted to cook for you, like I used to do. Kia is asleep, so it's just the two of us." She led me into the kitchen. "Remember how we used to sit at this table and talk about our future?" She paused, but not long enough for me to confirm. "We were so much happier then. I think if we want, we can get that back." She popped the tab on a beer and handed it to me.

"We've been through a lot. Maybe more than most couples, so we're bound to have ups and downs." I swallowed a mouthful of suds, groping for a way to tell her I didn't share her simplistic vision for our future. While she might not be upset about our new fiscal policy, I was still smarting about her indiscretion. And I was being nice by not calling it something much worse. It would be mean to tell her that Kia was the glue holding us together.

She pulled two plates from the oven and placed them on the table. The whole time she was biting her bottom lip.

"This smells good. I don't think you've cooked lamb chops in over a year." I took my favorite seat.

"You always do that." She only rested her index finger on the table, which meant in a minute she was going to be pointing it in my face. "I'm trying to have a serious conversation about us, about our relationship, and you want to talk about the food."

I shook my head. "If I didn't compliment you on your hard work, you would have pounced on me about my lack of appreciation. I can't win with you, Sasha." I picked up the knife and fork and cut into the meat. With a flip of her hand she pushed the plate beyond my reach.

"You can eat once we finish talking." She sat in the chair across from me.

"It'll be cold. If you didn't intend for us to eat yet, why'd you take it out of the oven?"

"Hear me out, Walter. Can you stop for just a few minutes and talk to me?"

181

I sighed, a let's-get-this-over-with sound, and put down my utensils. "Okay. Talk."

"I want us to be a family. It's the only thing I ever wanted. But instead of us growing closer, we seem to be drifting further apart. I think we should try harder for Kia's sake."

"Did you have these same thoughts while you were getting your kicks with Young Guy?" My voice was as serene as Kia's kiddie pool. But a rage still rolled in the pit of my stomach at the memory of Young Guy's finger buried inside of her. I was beginning to think that vision was never going to leave me, but I needed to work on it, because I was never going to leave her.

She nodded her head, but it wasn't in agreement. Her eyes darted around my face, first my mouth, and then she stared into my eyes. "If every discussion we have ends up in the same place, then I might as well pack up your stuff and put you out. Because if you think you're going to hold that against me forever, then you're wrong. I made a mistake. I'm sorry. Either move on or move out."

"I'm not leaving. I bought this house, remember?" The anger bubbling in my belly was hard to push down.

"Yeah, but your name isn't on the deed." She smirked with satisfaction.

Seconds ticked by and neither of us said anything. Her nostrils flared. She looked so determined we

182

weren't going to breeze through this topic like I hoped.

"Sasha, you've given this a lot of thought. So why don't you lay out your plan while I eat your delicious meal." A little flattery always warmed her up.

She pushed my plate toward me and positioned her meal in front of her. "First of all, are you going to bring up what happened on spring break every time we have a disagreement?"

"I don't know. I've wanted to mention it every few hours since it happened. But I didn't, so I think I'm doing pretty good." I chewed on a piece of lamb.

"Are you going to forgive me?"

"I'm trying."

"I guess that's all I can ask." She cut her lamb chop, but didn't eat it. "I want to get married. We had planned to, now we should do it. And I think if we're going to have any more children we should do it now. I'd like for our children to be close in age so they can play together. Besides, you're getting older and I don't want to wait four or five years."

The lamb stuck in my throat like a dry cotton ball. I'd planned my business trip to coordinate with my vasectomy recovery. Everything had worked out fine. The doctor said no sex for a week, so I'd planned my trip to be away from home and away from any questions. While I was in Denver, I'd followed the doctor's instructions to precision and it was easy. An honest man might have told his partner the truth, but I gave up on that virtue a long time ago.

I cleared my throat. "Get married, huh? How soon?" If I never respond to the second baby question, I'm not quite lying.

"I've never been married, so I want the whole shebang. I want the white dress, the white doves, the reception, and the band. I know you watch the checkbook like a hound and you've cut off my spending, but don't deny me this." She spun the expensive engagement ring I'd given her years ago, while I was still married.

"How soon, Sasha?"

"I was thinking around Christmas or early next year." She pushed her plate away. "You still want to marry me, don't you? Think about Kia. You don't want her to grow up and we have to explain to her why we're still shacking up."

To delay my answer I shoved another piece of lamb in my mouth. Being married seemed like such an odd idea for us now. I was content to live my life exactly the way it was. If I couldn't have Tracy, my current existence was fine with me. But my baby girl deserved more. That is, of course if she's mine. The test weren't back yet. But suppose she was and she grew up comparing her life to Crystal's. Would she hate me if she thought she'd come up short?

"Okay, let's do it." I even managed to smile. I could fake anything.

"Wow!" She jumped up and ran to my side of the

table, embracing me in the most sincere hug she'd probably given me in months. The only hug I could remember in a long time that wasn't tied to a large purchase. "I wasn't sure you were going to say yes. You've made me so happy." She practically sang the words.

"Don't go crazy, Sasha. You can have the wedding you want as long as it doesn't cost more than eighty thousand dollars. And not a penny more."

"Is that how much you spent on Crystal's wedding?"

"It doesn't matter, that's all I'm spending on this one." I stood up and put my empty plate in the sink. "Are you going to eat that?" I pointed at her untouched dinner.

"No, I'm too excited to eat." She hugged me again. "I think we ought to go upstairs and celebrate." She reached for my penis and for a moment I held my breath, expecting to feel sharp pains shooting through my loins from the vasectomy. When it didn't happen, I lifted her nightie and rubbed her ass.

I wasn't content unless I was trying to dig my life out of a hole. The deeper the pit, the more gratification I gleaned from my blunders. If I was so determined to tumble down that rabbit hole, there was at least one misstep I wasn't going to make again. And that was making another baby. But she didn't need to know that.

185

Chapter Twenty - Crystal

From the small kitchen sink, I stared out the grimy window that faced the brick building next door that also had grimy windows. The grass wasn't greener on the other side. If this condo had any view at all, then maybe living here would have been something to look forward to.

I dropped my cereal bowl on the counter and walked away. My cell phone lay on the corner of the small table we ate at, back when we used to eat together. Every time I walked near it, I couldn't help reading the text again. Without picking it up I could see the text was from Max. My fate was in the words spelled out on a mobile phone. The whole idea was too ludicrous for me to envision. We used to have something so beautiful.

Our appointment is tomorrow at 3:00 pm. Dr. Catherine Erickson. Her office is on 57th Avenue. Look it up. If you don't come, our marriage is over.

I guess I couldn't expect much more. He did find me with my tongue down another man's throat. But he wasn't one to sit in judgment. He'd done just as much. The way I figured it, we were about even. The slate could be wiped clean. He'd hurt me and now I'd done the same thing to him.

I found the simplest black skirt in my closet. The one that I could have worn if I was signing up to become a nun. The white button down blouse was just as boring. For the business I had to take care of today, this was the perfect attire.

The air in the condo grew thick, strangling me. It wasn't big enough to hold my guilt and the ghosts that seemed to fill every room. Even though Max was gone, there was enough of his stuff in the apartment to remind me he wasn't here anymore. I grabbed my purse, checked the address again, and hurried out the door. Getting outside was the only thing I could think about.

I walked the several blocks to 2nd Avenue. The only people crowding the street this time of morning were grim-faced commuters. Spring was so full of promise. I could almost make myself believe that any day now I was going to find the right path. I hadn't decided if I was going to show up at the appointment. I was never good at ultimatums nor was I so sure that saving my marriage was something I wanted to do. It sounded good, but it also had Tracy written all over it.

I hailed a cab. "Houston between Greenwich and Hudson, please," I said to the driver then settled back.

My actions made no sense, but nothing in my life did right now, so I was being consistent. The taxi driver made his way through morning traffic and I pretended I knew what I was going to say and do when I arrived at Dexter's studio.

At least there weren't any clients inside when I walked in. Dexter was focused on a drawing spread out on the long artist table. The bell chimed and he

187

pulled his attention away to face the door.

"Crystal." His face brightened when he turned and saw me. "I didn't...I wasn't expecting you." He dropped his pencil and rushed towards me. Before I could stop him, he hugged and kissed me.

I accepted his tongue. This was supposed to be a goodbye chat, but it felt so right. Dexter wanted me and I wanted him. Why couldn't I have this feeling with Max? He was my husband, the one who was supposed to be on this journey with me. Dexter was like a magnet. Without being able to explain the attraction, I only knew I wanted to be with him. In his company, I felt happy. It could have been the lack of baggage between us or because all we needed to do was kiss and not worry about all the other stuff.

When he took my hand, I didn't object when he led me to his private quarters. The room was bright. Every window blind was open, allowing the sunlight to pour in. Dexter released the buttons on my blouse and claimed my breasts. The heat from the sun warmed my back, but it was his tongue that made my temperature go up. He treated my body like one of his canvases.

I stepped out of my skirt and panties and pulled him to me. Lifting his t-shirt over his head exposed his fit physique, the one he worked so hard to maintain. I helped him out of his shorts. He wasn't wearing boxers or briefs.

"Are you always a renegade?" I asked.

"Count on it. I've never played fair." He kissed my shoulder, then my neck. Then he found the spot that Max could never seem to find. The spot that released all my inhibitions.

I ran my hand along his abs until I reached his erect shaft.

"Aww." He grabbed my hands and pinned my arms at my side.

"Let me." I wrenched free, kissing the firm hard line down the center of his chest. I dropped to my knees and took his erection. Dexter was always pleasing me and I wanted him to be filled with the buzz of pleasure, too. Besides, hearing the sounds coming from him made me feel superhuman. Bringing this six foot, three inch man to the point of weakness was exciting knowing I had that kind of power over him.

"Enough, Crystal," he said before removing a condom from the nightstand and rolling it on. He picked me up and placed me on the bed. When he eased into me, orange and red stars flashed behind my eyelids. Dexter matched my movements. I knew my actions wouldn't make sense to anyone, not even me. But it was as if I was addicted to him. When I wasn't with him, I wanted to be. And when we were together, it was as if I had no filters. He was even better than the fantasies I'd concocted. The way he strummed my body was pure bliss.

I wrapped my legs around his back and pulled

him in deeper until I was suspended over the edge of a cliff. I balanced there for what seemed like eternity. I could have stayed in that moment for the rest of my life and been happy. Dexter slowed his movements. He teased that spot, pushing me over the edge into ecstasy. He slammed into me one final time and I knew he was falling too.

He fell beside me on the bed. His breathing was ragged. Without opening my eyes, I could hear him remove the used condom.

"You know I didn't come here this morning for sex," I said without looking at him.

"Well, we know you weren't coming here to work. It's been over a week since I've seen you, so you had to know I was going to pounce on you. I think you like the idea that I can't resist you. Don't you?"

I kissed his forehead. "It does have a certain appeal." I bit my bottom lip, before climbing on top of him and kissing him again. If the moment could have been set in stone, then we'd always be able to share it. Letting him go wasn't something I was ready to think about. Maybe that time would never come.

I climbed on top of his penis.

He grabbed my hips, stopping my movements. "Crystal, don't. I don't have any more condoms. We have to stop." He was still, his teeth clenched.

Without releasing him, I bent down and kissed him, pushing my tongue beyond his tight lips. "Come on baby, you know you want me." I knew he was right, but I needed to be reckless, only if it was to prove I could.

"I do. But we shouldn't take this chance."

"Are you going to push me away?" I rotated my hips, grinding into him.

"You know I can't resist you. Damn it, Crystal." His body relaxed and so did his grip on my hips. He gave in to me and together our flesh pounded until we found the release we needed.

Thirty minutes later, we both were exhausted.

"You shouldn't have done that," he said while staring at me.

"Why, I know you don't have AIDS. Do you have an STD?" I was trying to be funny, but the serious look on his face made my stomach tighten.

"Worse. You could get pregnant. A baby never goes away, an STD you can clear up with a little penicillin."

"Like this isn't the first time we went bareback."

"I don't want to take chances." He pushed up in the bed to stare down at me.

I closed my eyes, unable to recognize myself. I was the good girl. Growing up, I never broke a rule, now I seemed to be looking for new opportunities to disgust myself. I was sleeping with the guy who was only supposed to be my fantasy. I had vowed never to step foot in my father's house of ill repute and I did. I wanted to ignore Marco for the rest of my life and yet

I'd poured my heart out to him. My path to self-destruction should have been more gratifying. And now, Dexter was the one pointing out my careless behavior. And I knew he was only one step away from being a playboy. My stomach felt like it was being punched from the inside.

"You're right. You're absolutely right. I'm not sure what I was thinking." I jumped out of the bed to gather my clothes. I was too ashamed to look at him.

"Don't get upset, Crystal. I just think we should be careful, that's all." Dexter talked to my back before I slammed the bathroom door on him.

I locked it and stepped into the shower.

"Let me in. This is not how I wanted to end our day." Dexter jiggled the handle.

"I've got to shower and dress. I've got an appointment." I yelled over the sound of the water, scrubbing my skin as if I could erase my guilt.

When I came out of the bathroom, Dexter was nowhere in sight. All I needed to do was retrieve my purse and get away from the crime scene.

I was halfway to his front door.

"Now you're trying to sneak out?" His voice was fraught with anger. "What is with you? You can't be mad because I've pointed out the obvious."

He only wore shorts, no shoes, no shirt. Having feelings for him was so easy. This had be the way Walter was tripped up by Sasha. I was willing to throw everything away to be with Dexter, and I was

192

on my way to see a marriage counselor.

The thoughts made me dizzy. I had to rest my hand on the sofa to keep from losing my balance. The room felt like it was moving in circles around me.

I didn't see Dexter cross the room, but I felt his arms around me, pulling me into a hug.

I pushed him away. "I'm not thinking clearly. I keep making one bad decision after another and I can't explain it."

"I'm just glad you're here. I didn't mean to upset you." He pulled me back into his chest and kissed me. The urgency in his tongue made me nervous. My knees started to tremble.

I moved away from him and walked to the other side of the room. I held up my hand, stopping him in place.

"I'm going to the counseling session," I said without looking at him. Instead I stared at my shoes.

"Why? Why would you put yourself through that?" The edge in his voice pulled my head up, locking eyes with him. "Do you really want to patch up your marriage? Because you know patches don't last long."

The blood in my veins ran cold. Tracy and Walter had tried to mend their marriage so many times, and in the end, none of it had worked. I was supposed to do everything just the opposite of Tracy, so why was I walking in her footsteps? Couldn't I at least be more original than either one of my parents? Instead of

193

agreeing with Dexter, I said, "I have to. I have to at least try."

"And what about me? Am I just supposed to forget my feelings for you? I think I'm falling in love with you, Crystal. Don't you understand that?"

His words wrapped around my heart like a cozy blanket. "Don't say that. It doesn't help."

"I don't give a damn about helping. What have we been doing these past few weeks? Am I just a test drive while you see if you like the single life? This is real for me and I'm being honest. I'm willing to fight for you. I think you feel the same way, but you're so scared of being like your mother or father you'd rather stay in an unhappy relationship than walk away."

He came to stand beside me. I looked up into his clear blue eyes and my breath caught. Everything he said was true, but it changed nothing.

"I've got to try, Dexter. I said those vows and they meant something."

He stepped away from me as if my words had slapped him. "Back then maybe they meant something. But look at everything that's happened. Can you tell me what just happened in my bedroom didn't mean anything?"

I refused to look at him. Instead, I circled the small desk we'd sat at several weeks ago. It was the before spot, before I lost my mind and started acting like my father's daughter. If Max knew what I was up to, would he be wounded like Tracy was by Walter? Would he then understand how his infidelity had ripped my heart out?

"What do you expect me to do? Wait? Sit here hoping you'll come back?" He turned his back on me. "I'm not that kind of guy. I've been wooing you for a year. I won't wait another year for you to make a decision."

Chapter Twenty One - Walter

I had to be the only man planning a wedding who would rather sit in the car in the driveway after work than go inside and pick out anything related to my upcoming nuptials. This had to be the second most ridiculous thing I ever did. Letting Tracy walk out of my life was the first. After two weeks, I thought my feelings about the wedding would improve. They hadn't. It wasn't the getting married thing that bothered me so much, it was the wedding thing that was chewing at me. Who plans a big wedding with a woman who can't be trusted?

At least now I knew I was never going to get over that. Her infidelity was the invisible scar I'd carry forever.

The front door opened and Sasha came out and walked towards me.

"I've been waiting for you to come home. You've been sitting out here for almost thirty minutes. Is something wrong?" Her eyes were wide, just the opposite of the set of her lips.

I opened the car door and stepped out. "I was just thinking."

"About who? You don't think I see you out here every day when you get home from work? You never pull up and get right out. You're always sitting out here thinking. Can you think in the house?"

I rubbed her back. "It's just work, Sasha, not

196

who." We had this same argument once a week. Her insecurity was escalating and my patience for dealing with it was declining.

"I have some ideas I want to run past you this evening." She reached for my hand and held it until we were inside. Our relationship shouldn't have been so painful. Sasha was almost twenty years younger than me. She had the flexibility of a gymnast and no sexual inhibitions. My brothers were always telling me how lucky I was, but they didn't have to endure the image of Young Guy pleasuring her. It was the one memory I couldn't get rid of. I couldn't remember where I put my wallet, but the moment I closed my eyes I could conjure up every frickin' detail of Sasha's indiscretion.

"Can we talk about it later? I'm sure whatever you decide is fine as long as you stay within budget." I dropped my briefcase on the floor and plopped in the recliner. "What's for dinner?"

She placed her hands on her hips and looked down at me. "I didn't have time to cook today. Kia wanted all my attention and I had a lot of errands to run. I want your input on the wedding." She pulled a box off the table and handed me two photo albums. "Which pictures do you like best?"

"I'm hungry and I want to eat, then I'll look at this stuff."

"There's pizza in the oven." She nodded her head towards the kitchen.

"Huh," I dropped the album on the floor and pushed out of the chair. "If you can't fix a proper dinner then I can't be bothered looking at those damn pictures. I've had a long day and I'm tired."

She jumped up and trailed behind me. "I'm sorry, baby. I'll cook a really big meal tomorrow. I promise. I got a little distracted today with all the stuff I need to do for the wedding." She opened the oven and placed two slices of cheese pizza on a plate. "We are going to be so happy. You just wait and see. Once we are married, we can have another baby and be a real family."

I nodded. If only getting married would solve our problems. I've been to that rodeo before and it's never as easy as I think it will be. I bit into the rubbery pizza that was only lukewarm. The road in front of me looked long and absolutely riddled with torture. It was the price I had to pay for being a cheat and having a baby daughter who deserved more than I could give her. If she ever sat down with Crystal and compared childhood notes, I didn't want her to come up short.

Sasha twisted the dishtowel through her fingers. Something was on her mind and if I asked what, she would suck me dry with some long drawn out tale.

"I'm exhausted. I'm going to bed." I threw the crust on the stained paper plate.

"You haven't even looked at the pictures. Do you expect me to pick the wedding photographer, too?"

She thumped her hand on her hip and threw me one of her perfected dirty looks.

"Does it have to be done tonight? Can't I do it in the morning?"

"Why do I get the impression you'd rather have all your teeth pulled without anesthesia than get married?" She spoke so slow it felt like a cold finger down my back. "You haven't done one thing to help. As a matter of fact, you're more distant than normal. Are you getting cold feet, Walter? Is that it?" She spat the words out like they were knives aimed right at me.

I sighed. There was no way around this topic. "I'd be just as happy to go to the court house and say I do. I don't need all the glitter and dazzle. Actually, I'd prefer to not have it." I slammed my palm on the table. "There, I've said it. Now you know."

"Oh, that's right. You and Tracy had the big wedding." Her sarcasm was unmistakable. Every time she mentioned Tracy, there was a hiss in her voice.

I took a deep breath and exhaled the anger bubbling in my gut. "I'm willing to fund the wedding. I want to get married to you. If you want me to get excited about roses versus calla lilies or chicken cordon blue versus chicken Marsala, it's not going to happen. You'll be a frustrated bride." I leaned into her face. "If you want to do this, then do it, just don't expect me to get all excited about it."

Tears sprang to her eyes.

"Save the waterfalls. It won't change how I feel."

"You're such a jerk. I don't know why I even want to marry you." She brushed past me, bumping my arm on her way out.

"I haven't changed." She was out of the room so I had to yell.

She stomped back towards me. Her eyes were narrow and her bottom lip trembled. "Well I have. And if you think I'm putting up with this bull then you're mistaken."

"What are you going to do, find another Young Guy to sleep with?"

Her face went blank. The tears stopped. "I'll take Kia and you'll never see either of us again, you bastard."

The beer was cold, the room was dark and the house was quiet. This was exactly what I'd wanted when I left the office. What I didn't want was the threat hanging around my neck like a noose. Sasha might be able to blackmail me with Kia, but she wouldn't be able to do it with another child. She didn't know, and I had no intentions of telling her, but I'd seen to that.

Sasha wasn't asleep. From the den I could hear her upstairs, slamming doors. I hoped she was enjoying her temper tantrum because it didn't faze me. My balls had been squeezed before, so she'd have to come up with a better threat if she wanted me to do something different.

I drained the suds from my third beer. Already, I was starting to feel better. Left to make the decision I wanted, I'd leave things the way they were. Our relationship was broke and a wedding wouldn't fix it.

It was a perfect evening to get shit-faced. I strolled into the kitchen, dropped the empty bottles in the recycle bin, and searched the cabinet for something harder. The bottle of scotch was hidden behind several sweet mixers that Sasha preferred. I pulled the unopened bottle from the cabinet, broke the seal and filled the glass halfway. Two ice cubes and I was set.

The last time I got buzzed was the night I saw Sasha and Young Guy. The woman was driving me to drink.

I settled back in my chair and sipped my scotch. The photo album was still on the floor where I'd dropped it. Why we needed to spend so much money on pictures we'd only look at once a year at most was about as ridiculous as burning money.

All the pictures looked the same. I closed my eyes and picked one. With the plaid book tucked under my arm and my drink in my other hand, I trudged up the stairs.

The door to the master bedroom was closed. Sasha wasn't going to make it easy. I tried the door and it was locked.

"Open up Sasha," I said.

"Like hell I will. Sleep on the sofa."

I leaned against the door. With my eyes closed I massaged the bridge of my nose without dropping the book. Maybe there was something to bachelorhood.

"I picked a photographer. I really like…" I pulled the book from my armpit and searched for a name. "Papell Photographics. See I'm trying."

She didn't reply but I could hear her moving around. Finally she unlocked the door and snatched it open. She made her way back to the bed without looking at me.

"You're such an ass, I don't know why I want to marry you."

"Because I'm absolutely adorable." I crawled in the bed beside her and managed to balance my drink.

"You're drunk."

"Not yet." I emptied the glass. It burned going down. "In a few minutes that declaration might be true. I'm working on a good one. I might even have a hangover in the morning."

She sucked her teeth before flipping over and pulling the sheet tight around her.

"I made a decision, so you don't have to be mad anymore." My words were slurred. If only I could solve everything with a few beers and a big shot of liquor. By now I should have been able to get life right, but it was still off on the horizon and my arms weren't long enough to reach it.

"I'm pregnant."

I laughed. She couldn't have said what I thought I heard. I struggled to push myself up in the bed. My head was already whirling. "That's not possible."

"Do you want to see the pee stick?"

"No, I want to meet the father."

Chapter Twenty-Two Tracy

I heard Marco's footsteps on the stairs. He was coming up to check on me again. Every few hours he peeked in as if I was a child that needed to be monitored. The way he tiptoed around me it was as if I was already sick. I knew he was trying to make me feel better, but all of the attention highlighted the trouble I was facing.

Instead of greeting him, I closed my eyes and pretended to sleep. The doctor said to go home and rest, and the results would be available in a week or so. If I just stayed in bed with the shades drawn the nightmare of the last week might go away.

"Are you awake?" His voice was gentle. The man never seemed to lose patience with me even though I was inconsolable. I was preparing for more bad news, refusing to be happy. If my life was going to change, the sooner I accepted my fate, the better.

I could feel Marco's weight on the bed. But I refused to open my eyes. Looking at him would only remind me of the life I might not have.

He placed his hand on my back. "You're going to have to eat something soon. And Crystal has called twice. She sounds worried."

Maybe I was being selfish, but I couldn't be any different. A few years ago I would have found relief in a vial of pills. I couldn't slip up and let that happen again, but the idea did occupy a lot of my thoughts.

204

"I'll be back shortly, Tracy. I won't let you push me away, so you ought to stop trying."

I heard the bedroom door close and I was alone again. When I was sure he was gone, I flipped over to stare across the room.

My goal wasn't to hurt him. I was trying to ease his pain. If I was going to be sick, vomiting, and losing my hair, I needed to give him an easy way to get out. According to my ex-husband, I could be quite bitchy and that was when I was well. I didn't want Marco to see the ugly side of me that was sure to come out if I had to fight to live.

Thinking about the could'a, would'a, should'a was exhausting. Until I knew how this was going to turn out for sure, everything I said and did would be fake. I was going through the motions.

Marco's voice drifted to me, but I couldn't make out his words. He was probably on the phone discussing my behavior with either Ursula or Carla. But he couldn't understand what I was going through. How much I stood to lose.

Before I could get up, Marco came back into the room. "I'm glad to see you're awake because you've got company. Carla and Ursula are here and I don't think they're going to leave any time soon." He hunched his shoulders.

I forced myself out of bed. Willed myself to get up and get out of the bedroom. "Tell them to give me five minutes, then they can come in."

205

After I raked a comb through my hair and added a little blush to my cheeks, I examined myself in the mirror. Even if Marco couldn't detect it, I could see the fear staring back at me.

Before I could make it out of the bedroom, my two best friends charged into the room. A woven picnic basket hung from Carla's arm and Ursula held a bottle of wine and three wine glasses. I had the dearest friends in the world and I knew they would always be there for me. They'd proven their love when they had to hold me together in those dark days back when I found out about Sasha.

"We're here to cheer you up." Carla flopped on the bed and Ursula perched on the opposite edge. "Ursula told me you were having a hard time. As your friends, here we are."

"Yep, we're going to drink a little wine, eat a little cheese, and tell a boatload of stories." Ursula popped the cork on the wine and filled the glasses.

"You don't have to do this for me. The last thing I want to do is bring you all down into this pit with me. Maybe I'm being silly and shouldn't worry, but I can't help feeling cheated somehow." I accepted the wine and crawled between the two of them on the bed.

Ursula pushed up on the pillow reserved for Marco. "You've been there for me as I cried in my pillow about Anthony, now I'm here for you."

"So, Ursula, what is going on with you and

Anthony? You don't think you'll get back together?" Carla snapped a plastic lid off a container of cheese squares and passed it to me.

"That man sucked up over a year of my life with his procrastination. Every time we talked about setting a date he turned green. I am so done with him." Ursula screwed up her face like she always did when this topic came up.

"Okay, I didn't mean to get you upset. We're here for Tracy. We'll plan another intervention for you on your own special day. I'm always looking for an opportunity to get out of the house and hang out with grown-ups." Carla held her wineglass up to mine and made a soft click.

"You guys are the best. Now what else do you have in that big basket? You wouldn't happen to have a cheese burger in there would you?" I tried to sound funny to lighten the mood. I knew they were trying to cheer me up and I loved them for their effort. But fear clung to me like an unwelcome housefly.

Carla picked up her handbag and pulled out her phone. "I've got just about anything you can think of on speed dial."

I almost spilled my wine with laughter. "No. I was only teasing. Now tell me about those adorable babies of yours."

Carla turned on her phone and spent the next several minutes showing us pictures from her photo gallery. Ursula tried to sound interested, but the

207

faraway look in her eyes was enough to indicate she was still hurting.

"I've got to call Crystal today. I know she's worried about me." I said.

"How is my goddaughter? I haven't talked to her in over a month." Carla leaned across the bed and refilled everyone's wine glass.

"She and Max are going through a rough patch. They're separated."

Carla shook her head. "The two of them were so happy. What could have gone wrong so fast?" Carla shoved a cracker smeared with Brie cheese into her mouth.

Even though Ursula turned away, I saw the look in her eyes that said she knew something more.

"What is it, Ursula? Have you talked to her?" I asked, pushing up higher in the bed and handing my full wine glass to Carla.

Carla set our glasses down and together we focused our attention on Ursula. My skin felt prickly. I couldn't accept any more bad news. "Has something more happened that I didn't know about? I'm her mother. What do you know?"

Ursula stood up. "I'm not going to betray her trust. If she wanted either of you to know, she would have talked to you. All I can say is she needs us right now." She turned to me and her voice trembled. "I know you're going through your own stuff right now, but—"

208

I held up my hand, stopping her from the hurtful thing she was about to say. I was being selfish, so worried about what was going on in my life, I wasn't there for Crystal. I was doing the exact thing I'd admonished Walter about just weeks ago. "You're right, you're right. No matter what, I've got to be there for her."

Ursula nodded with tears brimming in her eyes.

"Are you crying about Crystal or Anthony?" Carla turned to us. "I feel like you guys have left me behind. How come I don't know this stuff?"

"Because you've got enough on your hands with two little ones. Most days you've got baby brain." Ursula's edge was back. And just as quickly as the tears had showed up, they were gone.

There was a soft rap on the door and Marco stuck his head in. "Ursula, someone's here to see you."

Ursula's brow puckered. She looked at me as if I could verify what Marco just said. I shrugged my shoulders.

"Who is it? Why would someone come here...to…see me?" She began to stammer. "Who…"

"It's Anthony," Marco said.

For a moment we were all quiet, looking from one to the other like the reason he was here would somehow appear by magic.

Carla gave her a gentle shove toward the door. "You might as well go talk to him. Even if you don't like what he has to say, you gotta go out there."

Ursula bit her bottom lip.

"She's right. If nothing else, you can vent all your pent up anger at him. If you need us to come out there and beat him up, just yell." I bounced on the bed like a boxer.

"Yeah, well he doesn't have enough knees to beg on to make me change how I feel." Ursula rolled her eyes at us and left the room.

Carla and I spent the next hour finishing the bottle of wine and trying to guess what was going on in the other room.

"I better get going. Javier will need help getting the kids down for bed. He's a pushover, and if he gives them ice cream again tonight and I have to deal with them running around like wild banshees, I'm going to come back here and sleep in your spare bedroom." She packed up the basket, kissed my cheek, and left.

As soon as I was alone, I dialed Crystal. I should have done this sooner, but I was always so tentative when it came to discussing relationships. I knew she didn't think I had any advice to offer her.

Her phone rung five times before going to voice mail. I asked her to give me a call as soon as she could and hung up. Posed on the edge of the bed for what seemed like hours, I couldn't stay ensconced in the room another moment.

In the living room, Ursula and Anthony sat on chairs facing the fireplace.

"I'm sorry, I didn't mean to interrupt. Anthony, it's good to see you." It wasn't a lie. I liked Anthony and I thought he was good for Ursula. Settled her down. But he had one big flaw, eternal cold feet.

He came across the room and kissed my cheek. His bald head still looked odd. I never thought he was her type, but he had a quality that was somewhat mesmerizing. I actually thought he might be the one to get Ursula down the aisle. But judging from the set of her lips, whatever he was selling today, she wasn't buying.

"How are you?" Anthony said. He placed his hands in his pocket and stared at me. I could see Ursula shake her head. She hadn't told him about my situation.

"Well, you know—I'm just taking one day at a time." I stepped away from him. "I'll let you two talk." The tension in the room was noticeable. I just wanted to get away from their sadness. I had enough of my own.

"Marco went into his office," said Ursula.

I eased into Marco's den and closed the door, not wanting to disturb him if he was working or on the phone.

"Oh, you finally decided to come out of hiding. I knew if it was going to happen, your friends could get it done." He came toward me and kissed the top of my head. Afterward, he grabbed my hand and led me to the sofa. He sat on my right side. I'm sure he did that on purpose.

"So you knew, huh?"

"Of course. You weren't snoring."

I swatted at his shoulder, making sure to miss. "I don't snore." I laughed. Instead of hiding in the bedroom, I should have been out here with him soaking up his goodness.

"Tracy, I won't say I know what you're going through, but you can't push me away." He rubbed my arm.

I looked down at his massive hand. "I know, but I'm so afraid."

He pulled me closer, but his touch was tentative. Even though he was nowhere near the incision.

"I know. But you're not going through this alone. Don't make this harder for yourself than it needs to be."

"You're right. Tell me again how I got so lucky to have you."

"We've both paid our dues and we deserve something good," he said.

For several minutes, we sat in silence. With his arm around me, I could almost believe that I was going to get good news when the results of the biopsy came back.

"Anthony's been here for a long time. Maybe that's a good sign. I hope they can work out their troubles," I said.

"From the little bit I can gather, Ursula is not

giving him an easy time."

"She's no pushover. After what they've been through, I can't say I blame her.

Chapter Twenty-Three - Crystal

I think I held my breath from the time I left
Dexter's studio until I sat down on the bench in
Central Park. That first month when Max and I
moved to New York, the park was our favorite spot.
We'd grab a blanket and a sandwich from the corner
deli, sit on the grass and talk about how wonderful it
was to be on our own, in Manhattan. Back then we
thought we were invincible. Back then everything
was good. Then one day it all just seemed to
evaporate.

I had exactly fifteen minutes to make a decision
about the rest of my life. The exciting thing about
being a grown-up was supposed to be the freedom to
do what I wanted, when I wanted. I didn't have to eat
vegetables if I didn't want to, I could go to bed
whenever I chose, and if I didn't want to be pushed in
a corner, then I shouldn't have to accept Max's
demand to show up.

Months ago I would have jumped at the
opportunity to talk to someone who might be able to
put my marriage back on track. But that was before
Dexter escaped the bounds of my fantasy and became
so real I could smell and taste him even when he
wasn't anywhere near.

The menacing sound of Max's message on my
voice mail challenged me. It was almost as if he dared
me not to show up.

Several people occupied seats on the benches near me. On the end of the bench was a mother with a doublewide stroller with two sleeping babies. She seemed quite content to soak up the sun. I'm sure I must have looked pretty frightening. I ran out of Dexter's place so fast I didn't even comb my hair down.

I fluffed my curls and reapplied just enough lip gloss to hide any redness. The therapist's office was just across the Avenue, but from where I sat, it could have been a river between it and me.

This should have been easy. The opportunity to get my marriage back on track should have been my end goal. But I was more content to sit and allow the passage of time to make the decision for me. To actually show up at the counseling session was almost an admission of failure. It was something Tracy would have done.

My cell phone rang. I was inclined to ignore it, but it might have been Dexter or even Max. I was so mixed up I would have talked to either of them. Instead, I saw my mother's number and picked up.

"Hey Mom, I've been trying to reach you. How are you?" I used my fake voice to hide the anxiety that was churning in my stomach. Or was it guilt? I seemed to have an abundance of that lately.

"I'm fine. I don't have any results yet. That might take a week or so. But how are you? What's going on with you and Max?" There was tenderness in her

215

voice that assuaged my raw nerves. More than anything, I wanted to curl up in her lap and let her pat my head.

"I'm okay. It's just not a good day," I sighed. "I'm on my way to see a marriage counselor. Max's idea."

"That's a good thing. Maybe you two will work out your problems."

"I think our problems are too big and too deep for a few therapy sessions."

"Do you need me to come up there?"

"No."

"I will. I can be there in less than two hours." She was in her fix and repair mode, I could hear it in her voice.

"I know you would. But I have to do this all by myself. I promise to come home and have a long talk with you."

"Soon?" I could tell she was fishing for more information.

"Very soon. Now you promise me you'll call me as soon as you hear from the doctor."

"I promise. As soon as I know something."

I disconnected the call. With a deep sigh I stood. I couldn't pretend I had a choice. Like I told Dexter, I had to go to the meeting, at least the first one and see what would happen.

I trudged my way to the address Max had given me, feeling like I was slogging through several feet of

216

snow. At exactly three o'clock, I opened the door into the small waiting room to find Max seated with his foot resting on his knee, staring at his shoes. He didn't look up when I came through the door.

I contemplated where to sit. There was an empty seat beside him, but it felt as welcoming as a bed of nails. I took the chair across from him. For a moment, I held my breath. He looked as handsome as ever. His dark blue suit and crisp white shirt gave him an air of righteousness. After my stunt on the High Line, maybe he thought he'd earned the attitude. Compared to my skirt and now-wrinkled shirt, we were complete opposites. I half-expected him to be happy to see me, but he was more interested in his shoes.

"I didn't think you were going to show." He fingered the black shoelace dangling by his knee. His voice was flat.

"I didn't feel like I had a choice." There was no anger in my voice.

"You most certainly did. I thought I made that clear." He used the superior tone that he'd cultivated to sound important. I'd watched him practice it in the bathroom mirror. Back then, I thought it was funny, until he started using it on me. "I gave you plenty of time to make a decision." He squared his shoulders and expanded his chest, puffing up like a big bird. He was more courtroom than waiting room, and I wanted to run out the door and back onto the street. I knew we weren't going to accomplish anything. We both

217

were filled with too much contempt.

"Nothing about our relationship is clear."

He put his foot on the floor and stood. "What I saw on the High Line was very clear. I didn't imagine your tongue down the painter's throat, I saw it. So, while you were accusing me of screwing around, you were the one, huh?" He had the nerve to look hurt. I saw his eyes go cloudy before he turned his back on me.

The other door opened and a tall slender woman stepped in the room. "Hello, I'm Dr. Erickson." She held out her hand to Max.

"Hi, I'm Max and this is Crystal." He motioned toward me.

She waved us in. "Let's get started."

Her office was small, but cozy. There was a desk against one wall and an overstuffed sofa and chair on the opposite wall. The faded floral pattern might have been pretty several years ago. I imagined there were two seating choices just in case the husband and wife didn't want to sit next to each other. If they were happy, they probably shouldn't have a need to see a therapist. A box of tissues sat on the small end table, positioned between the sofa and chair.

I sat on the sofa, leaving plenty of room for Max beside me. He sat in the chair instead.

She turned the large leather chair around and faced us. "Okay, Max and Crystal, can you tell me why the two of you are here today?"

I folded my hands in my lap, set back on the worn out sofa and decided to keep my mouth shut. This was Max's idea, and after his accusation, I was curious how he was going to tell our story.

He coughed into his hand. "We've been having some problems. A lot of problems actually." He spoke slowly as if the chronology of how our marriage fell apart was the most important thing he had to do all day. "Crystal has become very suspicious. She's been following me around, interrupting client meetings, and just recently she's been kissing other men in public parks." He frowned at me. "That about sums it up, doesn't it, Crystal?"

Dr. Erickson turned her chair in my direction. "Let's hear what you have to say, Crystal."

I shot a glance at Max. Now I had to defend myself. "Max has a habit of slanting things in his favor. He forgot to mention he's never home. I spend more time alone than with him." I stared at Max while I talked. "He also failed to mention how he's been having an affair. Even though he thought he provided good excuses, I'm smart enough to know they're excuses and nothing more. And I don't kiss men in parks, I kissed one man, in one park."

"Okay," she said, before scribbling something into the pad balanced on her crossed knee. "Crystal, tell me a little about yourself."

The rest of the hour was spent without the two of us throwing allegations across the room like a volleyball.

"I have a little homework I want you two to do." She handed each of us a piece of paper. "This is a pretty easy assignment. I want you to write down what comes to your mind first. There are no right or wrong answers. We'll discuss your responses at our next session."

I nodded.

She pulled out a tablet. "Let's schedule something for next week."

When we were done I jumped off the sofa and rushed out the door. The small room was suffocating me. Without waiting for Max, I punched the elevator button to take me as far away as possible. Thankfully, the door closed before Max caught up to me. I didn't want to look at him. The session was as useless as I'd imagined it would be. Max admitted nothing and I felt like I was begging for him to love me. How pathetic.

On the street, I took a deep breath to minimize the pounding in my head. I rushed up 57th Avenue trying to outpace Max. I didn't want to see or talk to him. After the evil things he said in the meeting, I wasn't even sure I would attend another one.

In the taxi home, I rubbed my temples. The first session didn't go at all like I'd planned. Instead of giving us advice, she only asked a lot of questions. Why she needed to know how many siblings we had seemed ridiculous. I unfolded the assignment she'd given us both to do and examined it. We had to make a list of all the things we thought made a good marriage. Then on the opposite side of the page, make a list of all the things we thought was wrong with our marriage.

I sucked my tongue and crammed the paper back in my purse. How was any of this going to help us?

When I got home, I dropped my bag at the entry and made the three strides it took me to reach the kitchen. The half-full bottle of wine was a welcome sight. I removed the rubber cork and drank straight from the bottle.

I flopped on the bed. The ache in my head had begun to subside. I hadn't expected Max to be so angry. Did he think my guilt was any worse than his? I finished off the bottle of wine and contemplated getting another. There was no need to stay sober. If ever a situation required a drunken stupor, this had to be it.

####

I woke up the next morning with the hangover I'd courted the night before. Two empty wine bottles were beside me in the bed. The large wine stain on my shirt was evidence that I'd spilled a little. I put my legs over the edge of the bed, moving slow and steady. If I didn't try to make any sudden movements, I'd be fine.

Yesterday, neither Max nor I had taken the time to

greet each other. I say hello to strangers on the street or subway, but I walked into an office, looked at the man I married and vowed to love and honor, and never even said hello. And he was guilty of the same bad manners. What had happened to us? How could our love evaporate? Living with Walter and Tracy should have prepared me for this situation.

Chapter Twenty- Four - Walter

It doesn't take long for something to become a habit. I used to pull in the drive way and run into the house. Getting to Sasha was the only thing that interested me. But now, I turned off the car and gathered my thoughts before going in.

There was never any guarantee what would be waiting for me when I walked through the door.

Since Sasha had told me she was pregnant, going in the house felt more like stepping into a boxing ring than a home. Whenever we decided to talk, I'd square off in my corner and she'd square off in hers and the bickering circus began. She refused to tell me who the lucky father was, instead she wanted to pin it on me.

I pushed the driver seat back, closed my eyes, and listened to the end of a song by Kem. With each note he hit, I tried to exhale, to release the tension in my shoulders. The last thing I needed was another anxiety attack, but the pressure building in my chest was familiar. Like an old friend stopping by for a visit and staying much too long. I ignored the pressure and tried to brush away the thoughts of what happened the last time I felt this way. The emergency room had become a distant memory and I didn't want a repeat performance.

One thing I knew for sure, Sasha wouldn't come out to greet me. She hadn't said more than ten words to me since I refused to gush over the baby announcement. She was excellent in giving me the cold shoulder. For such a petite woman, she sure had the chilling powers of an ice princess. But I had right on my side. I was fixed, so this time she might have outsmarted herself.

I shut down the car, exhaled one more time, and headed inside. Tonight we'd resolve this. We didn't need to wait nine months for another blood test. I didn't want another baby, and if someone forced me to be truthful, I'd probably admit that having Kia was an accident. But that was something I'd keep buried forever. No child wanted to hear they were unwanted. I had eighteen years of growing up unwanted on the red clay of Georgia to attest to that.

The house was quiet. A welcome sound under normal circumstances, but this wasn't a peaceful silence. This absence of noise was coated in ice. The kind that drove a wedge that can never be mended between two people. If I wanted to protect Kia, I needed to find a way to handle my anger. If Sasha could just admit she'd cheated with someone other than Young Guy, then maybe we could find a way to make things right. Maybe we'd never be able to go back to that first blissful year when all we did was make love and plan for a future that was never going to happen, but we could cobble together some kind of truce that would allow the children to grow up unscarred by all of our crap.

I dropped my briefcase on the floor and my keys

on the entry table. If Sasha was too young and naive to understand what we needed to do, then I had to be man enough to do it for us.

I made my way upstairs, into Kia's room. She was sprawled out on her back, sound asleep. Her lips were puckered into a perfect 'o'. I ran my finger along the soft skin of her cheek. This little one I could be proud of. How so much perfection was fit into such a small package still amazed me. My heart swelled every time I looked at her.

Careful not to wake her up, I backed out of the room and pulled the door closed. I went downstairs and found Sasha seated at the kitchen table, reading one of her romance novels, a carton of day-old Chinese food in front of her. I parked myself in the chair in front of her and folded my hands on the table.

"We can't keep on this way, you know? We need to talk."

She flipped the page with so much force she ripped it.

"Are you going to pretend I'm not trying to talk to you?" I tried to use the same tone I had to use at work to convince customers to trust me. I'd practiced the negotiating tactic for years, never realizing how handy it would be in my personal life.

"I think you've said enough already. You've made yourself perfectly clear, and unless you want to take back some of the stuff you've said, I think we better keep this stealth silence going."

225

We'd been arguing for over a week, which only made Sasha more stubborn and made me angrier. Tracy and I may have had a few rough patches, but nothing like this. Sasha seemed to thrive on discourse. She looked me in the eye and expected me to believe I was the father of the baby she was carrying. Somehow, we managed to reserve our modulated shouting for when Kia was sleeping or off on some playdate. That little girl with my smile was the only thing keeping me here.

I stood and strolled around the table while she pretended to eat leftover Chinese food and ignore me. With each stride, the tightness in my shoulders grew more intense. I vowed to come to some resolution before the end of the night, but she was still sticking to her story. I exhaled through my nose without drawing her attention.

"I've said some things I probably shouldn't have and so have you. But I think if we can put our feelings aside, we just might be able to come to some resolution." The calm timbre of my voice was the polar opposite of the storm raging just below my surface. I shoved my fists in my pockets.

She lifted her eyes to look up at me without raising her head. "I don't talk to jackasses."

"And I don't want to be planning a wedding with a cheater. But look where we are." Already my tone was as harsh as hers.

She rested her chin in her palm. "You are a

cheater too, remember? That's why we're together. Let's call Tracy and ask her where she'd classify you? You jerk."

I exhaled and sat back down. This bickering was getting us nowhere. "Why don't we stop calling each other names? We should be able to have a grown-up conversation without insulting each other. I'm trying to be reasonable."

"Like hell you are."

"I've counted the weeks. You said your period was two weeks late." I kept my voice level like I was ordering pizza. Biting back the urge to say she wasn't known as Ms. Faithful.

"I can think of a bunch of things I'd like to call you right now." She banged her palm on the table. She hit the tip of the fork and sent shrimp fried rice across the table. "I told you the other night and I'm only going to say this one more time. What happened in Nassau was a mistake. It only happened that once. You ought to know all about blunders. You think I don't know I'm your major mistake? I see it in your eyes, Walter. You look at me hoping to see your ex-wife. The hesitant way you reach for me now. I'm your second choice and I know it. I live it. The only time you're open to me is when we're having sex. And even then, do you know how many times you've called me Tracy?" Her voice edged up. She didn't cry easy, but she was on the verge. Maybe her hormones had started to change already.

227

"The least I can do right now is be honest with you." I swallowed the pit lodged in the back of my throat. "I sometimes wonder if maybe I've ruined both of our lives. And now we have a baby. I wish I knew how to fix things, to get us back to where we used to be, but I don't." I spoke slowly to ease the harshness of my confession.

She sniffed and began gathering the rice that had scattered across the table, picking up one grain at a time.

We sat that way for several moments, until all the food was back in the cardboard container. It was probably the most meaningful moment we'd had together in months.

"So now what?" she asked without looking at me.

"I don't want to live a life of lies. I have my doubts, Sasha."

"And there is nothing I can say that will convince you. One day you're going to realize that whatever it is you're looking for, you already have. You threw away your relationship with Tracy, I just hope you won't be foolish enough to throw this one away, too."

I hunched my shoulders. "We'll just have to wait and see, I guess."

"What does that mean?" Her eyes grew dark and narrow.

"When the baby is born, we'll do a paternity test."

She covered her mouth. Her hand trembled. My words severed something between us.

"If that's what you feel is necessary, then that's what we'll do. The wedding is off." There was no malice in her voice. She spoke as calmly to me as she did with Kia, but I heard what she didn't say. It was like ice cracking in some far off place like the Arctic. She pushed away from the table and tipped over the chair.

I stood and followed her out of the room. "Sasha, I had a vasectomy about four weeks ago. That trip to Vegas was for my recovery. I can't be the father. That's why I'm pushing this. I think if you just tell the truth we can make some progress. I'll still be here, you'll never have to worry about finances and I want to play a role in Kia's life, not just an every-other-weekend kind of father."

She stopped and turned to me. Her breathing was rushed and labored. I watched her chest expand.

"You rotten bastard. Is this some kind of trick?"

I shook my head. "I know you wanted another baby, but honestly, I didn't. I'm getting too old. Babies are for younger people. I should be planning my retirement not thinking which daycare has the best mid-day snack."

"So all that talk about getting married and being a family, that was just my pipe dream and you let me go on and on like you were in agreement."

"It's not like we don't have any children. We have Kia."

"But you weren't going to tell me that you'd done

229

this thing?" There was anger in her voice now.

"No."

She sucked her tongue, her hip shoved out to one side. "I'm going to keep my mouth shut right now, because with all the emotion racing through me, I know I'm going to say something that I might regret." She turned around with a calmness that seemed to appear by magic and walked out of the room as if our lives weren't all torn up.

Chapter Twenty-Five - Crystal

It wasn't until the day of our next counseling session that I knew for sure I was going to go. I watched the bedroom gradually grow brighter as what little sunlight that managed to find its way between the tall buildings found its way into the room.

My self-imposed sobriety from the last week had only been partially effective. No wine and no Dexter. But I still craved them both. I kept my promise to myself to ignore Dexter's calls, and the one time he showed up announced at my building, I pretended not to be at home.

Before getting out of bed I dialed my mother. "Good morning, how are you feeling this morning?"

"Hey baby, I'm doing fine. I'm not nearly as sore this morning."

"I don't have plans for this weekend, I could come down and help take care of you." There was no need to tell her I was actually looking for a place to run to. If I was in Delaware I could pretend my days weren't long and empty and filled with nothing but regret.

"Crystal, I know you're busy. You don't need to call me every morning." The calmness in her voice was amazing. I don't think I could have waited to see if my life was going to be upended and remain as tranquil as she was.

"I want to. I'm worried about you. Besides, it's

231

not like I'm rushing out the door to anything else this morning." I lay back against the pillow. "Any word yet?"

"No, the doctor says I should know soon. I'm hoping to hear something by the end of the week. This waiting is driving me nuts." There it was, the anxiousness I hadn't heard before.

"You'll call me as soon as you know something, right?" I asked.

"Of course I will," she said. But Marco would know first. I shouldn't have been jealous of him, but I was. It was like sharing my mother with a stranger and the idea still felt scratchy.

I picked up the phone to dial Dexter. I wanted to hear his voice. Maybe before going to the counselor I could stop by for another quick visit. I put the phone down. Sooner or later I needed to stop fooling myself.

The day slipped by with mindless hours of daytime television and several trips to the refrigerator. I kept eying the bottle of wine, but I opted for the water instead. If I had to discuss all the things wrong with my marriage, I needed to do it with a clear head and without the lingering reminders of mind-blowing sex with someone whom I should have had the sense to know was off limits.

I found the homework assignment and placed it on the table in front of me. It wasn't easy listing those things that made a good marriage. I didn't have an example to draw from. The other side of the paper was much easier to complete. I could answer a million different ways. When did I think the trouble began? Was it that first night when he came home late, creeping into the house like I'd heard my father do so many times, or was it when I overheard the conversation where his voice was hushed and tender? It could have been the absence of our sex life or his absence in the house. There were so many choices I almost wanted to give the counselor a multiple-choice selection.

By the time I made it to 57th Avenue, my palms were moist. I stepped off the elevator and stood outside the suite. I paused long enough to take a deep breath. I didn't know what the outcome was going to be for this session, but what was even scarier, I was ready for it to be behind me. Just thinking about the sessions was worse than attending them.

"Aren't you going in?"

I jumped and turned to find Max standing behind me. He was dressed in his work attire, his favorite dark blue suit still looked crisped. The powder blue shirt that he always wore with that suit was unbuttoned at the collar and his tie was crooked. I wanted to reach over and straighten it. But touching my husband was foreign to me now. We'd become strangers.

I wanted him to reach for me and kiss me.

To say he missed me.

To say he loved me.

233

To say something intimate to me, like lovers do when they've been apart for a long time.

But the moment evaporated when he cast his gaze away, down at the dull brown carpet. And the fear of his reaction kept me from reaching for him.

"No. I'm just preparing. Hopefully this session will be more purposeful than the last."

He reached around me to open the door. It was the nicest gesture he'd done for me in months.

In the counselor's office, we assumed the same positions on the opposite sides of the room, just like the week before.

"Good afternoon, Max and Crystal." She looked at each of us in our prospective corners. "I have a request this morning and please let me know if it makes you feel uncomfortable." She waited a moment and my pulse quickened.

Max crossed his foot over his knee and looked at her. He must have had the same uncomfortable feeling crawling up his spine.

"I'd like for the two of you to sit on the sofa next to each other. I'm not asking you to hold hands or to do anything intimate, simply sit beside each other. Do you think you can do that for me?" Her question hung on the tension in the room.

Max uncrossed his leg and came to sit next to me. There was enough space between us for a small child, but still I could feel the heat rising from his body. Max was stiff, his hands were in his lap and his feet were stationed on the floor.

"Thank you, Max," she said. "Now were you able to complete the assignment I gave you?"

Without waiting for Max to respond, I said, "I did." I removed the crumpled paper from my bag and unfolded it.

"Good, Crystal. How about you Max? Did you answer the questions?" Her voice was calm, no accusations attached to it.

"No. I was busy at work and I thought the exercise was pointless."

"I see." She scribbled something on her pad. Hopefully, I was getting credit for the work I'd done and he was getting a big fat zero. This had been his idea.

"Crystal, can you share your answers with us?" she asked.

After a deep breath, I read the questions and my responses. Being careful not to look at Max as I did.

I half expected her to grade my answers, but she only nodded. "Max would you mind at least sharing what you would have written if you'd had the opportunity."

He sat forward, placing his elbows on his knees. "I've never mistreated Crystal. The only thing that I'm guilty of is working hard to make a better life for the two of us. I didn't want her to have to worry about not finding a job. I know she hates the condo we're in and I wanted to be able to move us somewhere nicer.

But she is so…so…stuck on what happened to her parents… It seemed like she wanted to push me away."

"How can you say that," I jumped in before the counselor could reply. "I was always begging you to spend time with me. To call me. But the more I asked, the less you did. I just wanted you to come home at a decent time so we could act like a normal married couple. Instead, you turned me into my mother, begging for affection."

Silence fell over the small office. My childlike rant reverberated across the room.

"Max would you like to respond to what Crystal just said?" The counselor asked.

He turned to me. "You hate the condo, Crystal." His words were an assault.

"Yes," I admitted. "But I didn't want it to come between us. Don't try to pin this whole mess on me. It has nothing to do with where we live." I bit my tongue. I'd promised not to have an outburst today and five minutes into the session he'd managed to bait me.

"Look, my father worked hard to take care of his family. He put us in a nice house, took us on nice trips, and paid for college tuitions. I just wanted to be able to do the same thing for my family. Instead, all I got was a bunch of accusations and innuendos every evening when I got home."

I took a deep breath. "From the time I was in

236

grade school my father always had an excuse for his behavior. It was work. It was his upbringing. All those times I sat on the stairs just out of their line of vision while they argued about the other women and the excessive work hours. My mother always took him back. Forgiving him. And for what? So that he could go off and start another family and leave her anyway." The words were as distasteful to say as conjuring up the memories were. "I'm not going to be a fool for you, Max. I don't want to waste years fighting for the marriage I want. If you want to throw it away, let's do it now. Don't wait until I'm in my forties."

He jumped up from the sofa and looked at me through narrow slits in his eyes. "Maybe we've wasted your time, Dr. Erickson. Crystal has her view of the world and nothing is ever going to change it."

I crossed my arms over my chest and huffed.

"Max, please take a seat. Sometimes you get more done when you get to the emotional reasons of why you're here."

"I won't let her put all this on my shoulders. I've been faithful. I know how much the split between her parents hurts and I would never want to inflict that kind of pain on her. Ever. But there she is, in the middle of New York kissing another man. How can you explain that, Crystal? How do you think I feel? Always being so careful, having to tiptoe around your feelings. I'd rather cut off my right arm than to hurt you. On all that is sacred in my life I have never been unfaithful to you. The thought never once crossed my mind and then…" His words choked off and he turned his back to me.

"Well, you did it first. Besides you walked out on me. Did you think I was going to sit at home waiting for you to come back like some sick puppy?"

"I didn't expect you to cheat on me. Our marriage wasn't over." He walked back to the sofa and bent toward me. "Did you sleep with him, Crystal? Please tell me the truth because I'm pouring my heart out here for you. Just tell me the truth." The words sounded like they were being wrenched from his body.

I closed my eyes and the last vision of Dexter between my legs came to life. My flesh grew warm all over, moistening my blouse and my armpits. I could keep my secret buried or I could try to break free from the shame coating me. "Yes." The words were barely audible, but the way Max staggered back, I knew he heard me. For just a moment, I thought he was in shock. His face went blank. Then he took a deep breath before walking out of the office and slamming the door.

Chapter Twenty-Six - Tracy

I thought it was impossible to go back to work, cook dinner or make love with the threat of my future so undetermined. But I did. If it weren't for the unexpected soreness under my left arm when I moved it in certain positions, I could have almost forgotten the invasion. But this morning, while we sipped coffee before going to work, the phone rang and reality came rushing back.

"Good morning Ms. Ferrara, Dr. Jefferies would like to know if you can come in for an appointment sometime today." My whole body began to shake. Marco was by my side in an instant, holding on to my arm, supporting me.

I dropped the phone and plopped into the chair. Marco picked up the receiver and continued the conversation. My mind rushed through all the people I would miss, all the things I'd never get to do, the grandchildren I'd never get to hold and spoil. I made my way to the sofa, pulled a pillow to my stomach and tucked into a tight ball. The fight to keep the anguish from consuming me, killing me long before the ravages of cancer ever could, was the only thing I could focus on. All at once I was both hot and cold.

"Arrestare, bella." Marco found a small space next to me on the sofa and gathered me into his arms. "You don't even know what she's going to say, you mustn't do this." He spoke with urgency.

239

"Marco, the only time they call you into the office is to tell you bad news. No doctor wants to spend time talking to a healthy patient. There's no glory in that."

"That can't be true in all cases. The call can't always mean bad news." I don't know if he was trying to convince himself or me. And I had no response for him.

"What time do we go?"

"She wants to see us in an hour," he said.

"I don't think I can do it, Marco. How can I?" I was almost crying. There was a lump that extended from my throat to the bottom of my stomach.

"You don't have to do it alone. You're never going to be alone." He squeezed me so tight I could almost believe that having him beside me was going to make things better.

Chapter Twenty-Seven - Crystal

The small condo seemed to shrink a little more every day. It didn't help that I refused to leave it for more than a few minutes at a time. Whatever I needed, I had delivered. A luxury in New York that I used to its fullest advantage.

On the sofa next to me was a pile of corn chips, nesting on a paper towel. This was my dinner, which went so nice with the corn flakes I had for breakfast. I looked down at my thin legs. I couldn't afford to lose another pound, but my appearance was of no interest to me. The guilt chewing at my insides was more harmful than the lack of nutrition. There were only two things I continued to be consistent about. Calling my mother every morning and dialing Max every evening when I thought he'd be home from work. Mom picked up every time. Max did not.

It was eleven, the nightly news was coming on the television and still there was no answer from his ringing phone. I should have lied. Telling him I slept with…made love to…had sex with Dexter, served no purpose. It was something I could have kept to myself forever. And I should have. The crushing hurt on Max's face before he walked out was too much to bear. I thought I wanted to strike out at him, but the result had backfired on me.

Dexter must have dropped off the earth. He no longer found it important to call my number daily. I wouldn't have been surprised if someone else had come along who was appealing to him and hopefully more available. I couldn't even conjure up a new fantasy of him anymore. But I'd always have the passionate memories that lingered in my head like old movie reels on a consistent loop. Only now they were all a little tarnished because of the havoc that was created to make them.

The sound of a key in the lock made me scramble off the sofa, sending corn chips flying onto the floor. I looked around for something to protect myself, a weapon. The remote wouldn't have deterred anyone, but it was the only thing of substance I saw.

Max stepped through the door. Our eyes locked for a moment and I felt the stirring for him that I thought had disappeared like everything else between us. The confidence he wore like his expensive suits was missing. He looked like a man looking for something and exhausted from the search. But my soul saw the man I used to breathe for. Crippling regret surged through my veins, leaving a stain that would never disappear.

"I wasn't expecting you," I said. "I wasn't expecting anyone." I wore the same clothes from the day before. The milk stain from this morning seemed even larger and more noticeable now as I looked down at my ragged appearance. My tangled curls hadn't been combed since yesterday. What was the use, nobody was here to see me.

"No, I guess you weren't. But since I'm still paying the mortgage, I figured I didn't need to call in order to stop by." There was no bitterness in his voice or resentment guarding his face. Even though he looked groomed, something about him was unkempt.

We stood in the small living room, him on one side by the door, me next to the sofa on a bed of chips. Strangers. Much like we had been at that first counseling session. My heart raced and I was almost unsteady on my legs. He was coming to ask me for a divorce. I could see it in his shoulders. The uncharacteristic slump announced the weight he was struggling to bear. I wanted to stay his words. If it had to come, I just didn't want it to be now. When I envisioned this moment, we were always seated in a restaurant, acting like a civilized couple. Afterward, I imagined he'd kiss my cheek and squeeze my hand before walking away.

I wanted to stop him from saying those words. Not today. I wasn't ready. I needed more time. Once they came out of his mouth he wouldn't take them back.

My head felt light and my mouth began to water. I was too weak to focus and then my body faltered. A sense of peace surrounded me like a band of fairy godmothers and then everything went black.

####

243

I opened my eyes, not focusing on anything. For a few seconds, I laid very still. Trying to gather my thoughts. I had the sensation of looking down on my life. With just a few tweaks I could move this piece a little to the right, and turn that piece over, and everything would fit perfectly together like a puzzle.

It was important for me to pull it together. What was going on? Max was here. Something bad was about to happen. I scrambled to sit up. I was lying in the bed, in the dark bedroom.

Max was perched on the edge of the bed gazing over the headboard, at the painting. Dexter's painting.

"You fainted," he said without adjusting his focus.

He was still here. I blinked. The only light in the room came from the alarm clock, a soft green glow that made his face look even sadder.

"You know, I never liked that painting and I never understood why it had to go in this room. It made no sense to me back then." He laughed. But there was no joy in it. It was the hard kind of chuckle that peopled used to mask their pain. "Were the two of you going at it back then?"

"No."

"How about all those mornings you all jogged together? You can tell me now since we're telling the truth."

"Max, it wasn't like that ever." I never knew talking could be so painful. "While we were together,

I never did anything. But you left me."

"You drove me away. I don't understand why you have to destroy the people who love you. You've treated your mother so badly and you have almost no relationship with your father. All you need now is a deserted island and I think your mission will be complete."

I hugged my arms around my waist and rocked back and forth.

"That's not true." I whispered. "My relationship with my parents is complicated."

"All relationships are complicated. But that doesn't mean you throw them away."

"Okay, I get it, I'm damaged."

We sat, neither of us talking. When we first married, moments of comfortable quiet used to bring me joy and allowed me to bask in the happiness burning between us. But now I could almost hear the wretched sound of our marriage being ripped apart.

I couldn't bear it. "I've been calling you."

"I know. But I wasn't ready to talk." He continued to stare at the mural.

I didn't know this Max. He seemed different. I wanted to tell him it didn't mean anything. I wanted to tell him I was sorry. I wanted to tell him we could fix our marriage. Everything I wanted to tell him was lodged in my throat, too big, too important, and too meaningless to change the past.

"You didn't come to our therapy session last

week. I was worried."

He stood up, finally breaking the connection with the painting. "I had some soul searching to do and it wasn't going to happen in Dr. Erickson's office." His voice was low, his back was to me. I had to strain to hear him. "Do you love him, Crystal? Dexter, are you in love with him?"

It wasn't the question I was expecting. And I didn't want to be flippant with my answer. He deserved more. Our lives were scattered across the bedroom like yesterday's garbage and now it was time to clean up the mess. No matter what we decided to do next, this moment required the truth. The whole ugly mess that I'd been dodging and ignoring.

"I think some part of me did. He gave me the attention I thought I needed." I paused. Just hearing the words caused my body to ache and I'd already hurt Max enough. "But it's not the kind of love to build on. I know now that it was the passing fancy kind. The kind you get when you see a new pair of shoes that you think you need to have."

He made a strangled sound. "You gambled our lives on something that didn't mean any more to you than a pair of shoes."

"That's not what I was saying. It was only an analogy. I never wanted to hurt you." I sat up on my knees.

"I know what an analogy is. Let me give you one. I was working my ass off to give you a better life.

Trying to fill the shoes of your father, making sure his little girl never wanted for anything." He jerked around and narrowed his eyes on me. "I just didn't know you were walking in his footsteps, too."

He should have just hit me. I think it would have been less agonizing.

"For the last few weeks I've been trying to determine if I can walk away. I've almost convinced myself I can. I really want to," he said.

"Max, I thought you were cheating on me. The missed dinners, the blond you seemed too familiar with. I was hurting, too."

"Don't you dare." The anger in his voice startled me. "You had a choice and you made a bad one. The least you could do is own it."

I climbed off the bed and went to him. "I know. You're right." I reached for his shoulder and he pulled away. "There has got to be a way for us to fix this. I still love you, Max. I always will."

His face contorted as if my words had inflicted a new pain on him. "If that should make me feel better, it doesn't. The only reason I'm standing here, now, is because I think you…I think your parents' relationship had something to do with all of this. I can't help but believe if your family wasn't so dysfunctional, this would have never happened to us."

"Can't you see I'm messed up? You promised to love me for better or worse, remember?"

He rubbed his forehead and closed his eyes. "I

247

thought worse would be some bad meatloaf or you'd get sick and I have to nurse you back to health. I had no idea you'd purposely try to destroy me."

I dropped my hand to my side. Placing all the blame at my parents' feet would have been so easy, my ticket to get out of jail. But I should have been able to control my impulses. Nothing I ever read said infidelity was hereditary. The only thing I had was a bunch of words and they couldn't heal the wounds we suffered from. Sometimes the pain went too deep to ever go away.

"Why were you calling me?" He seemed to detach from the discussion, switching to the all-business person I'd come to resent. But I couldn't fight him on this. I was so busy being hurt and self-righteous, I'd hurt the person I cherished most in this world.

I inhaled, trying to compose my thoughts. "If you're not going to come to therapy, what are we going to do?" Just asking the question made my head swoon. This was his opportunity to end it all.

"I don't know. I don't want to think about it right now." He stared at me for a long time, almost saying something but stopping himself. After what seemed like forever, he turned and left the bedroom. His shoes made a soft sound on the wooden floor. Then I heard the entry door close.

Chapter Twenty-Eight - Walter

We had established our own version of the cold war. Sasha existed on her turf and, when I was home, I stayed on mine. As much as I hated it, Kia was stuck in the neutral territory—the kitchen. We sat together at night eating whatever Sasha prepared or ordered in, and instead of talking to each other, we focused all our attention on Kia. After entertaining us through a meal, Kia was exhausted and irritable and ready for bed.

The house was still. From the living room I could hear the dull drone of the television. This couldn't be good for any of us. It was like living in a morgue. While I was trying to do the right thing, maybe I was causing more harm. Kia should be in a place with happy people fussing over her.

When Sasha came downstairs from putting her to sleep, maybe we could find a new normal until we resolved our dilemma.

Sasha walked by me and went into the kitchen. I'm sure she refused to look at me on purpose.

"Is she asleep?" The deep pitch of my voice in the quiet house sounded sharp and out of place compared to the dainty conversations Sasha had with Kia. The exaggerated happiness that Sasha exhibited when playing with the baby I'm sure was meant to hide the sadness looming just above our heads.

She gave me a long stare before responding.

"Yeah." She began to clear the table.

"Can you sit down for a minute? I think we need to talk," I said.

Not until everything was off the table did she flop into the chair next to me, resembling an angry teenager called in for punishment.

"I think we're being selfish to Kia." I cleared my throat. "For her motor skills to develop properly, she needs to hear conversations."

Sasha glared at me without registering my remarks.

"I know I'm just as guilty of this as you are, but for her we need to do better."

She stood up and busied herself at the sink. "I have an appointment with the doctor tomorrow. I want you to attend with me," she said without emotion.

"Why, what does that have to do with the conversation we're having?" I tried to control my anger. The two of us always managed to be on different topics.

"It has everything to do with this conversation. I'm not going to wait nine months to resolve our situation. Living in a house with this much stress is not good for me, the baby, or Kia."

"You're going to have an abortion?" I was standing now, my voice elevated. "You can't do that."

She placed a glass in the dishwasher then turned

to me. She looked the same. Still petite and youthful, but her lips had settled into an unhappiness that was always present, even when she was laughing with Kia. "No, I'm not," she said with disgust. "We're going to talk to the doctor about a DNA test. I want to get this over. Now."

"Is that possible?"

"I've done some research and the answer is yes. I want to get this over with. I refuse to live with this weight hanging over my head and with you looking down your nose at me as if I'm some accident the dog had on the carpet."

"I never meant to make you feel that way. I was only being honest with you."

She placed her hands on her still narrow waist. "Well, maybe I should thank you for your honesty, but then that wouldn't be very honest of me."

"What time is the appointment?"

"First thing in the morning. The sooner we can get this over with the better. The doctor will describe the process to us tomorrow and hopefully we can schedule the procedure in a day or two. Once we get the results, you can pack your bags and find somewhere else to live."

Her words took a moment to have any meaning to me. "So, was that an admission? If it was then we have the answer we're looking for."

Her facial expression grew menacing. "Why would I want to live with a man who thinks so little of me? Why? I'll tell you why. I want to prove to you that I'm telling the truth. I just want to vindicate myself." She spun around and left the room, returning to her neutral ground.

####

I kept my head buried in a parenting magazine while we waited for Sasha's name to be called. Being the only man in the waiting room made me more uncomfortable than usual. The stigma of suspicion radiated from my pores like a new fashion scent. Sasha's indignation was hard for me to accept. This was her mess, she'd created it. Her inability to understand why I had doubts—big doubts baffled me. If she had any idea how much angst I'd had over Kia's parentage, maybe she'd understand why I found this necessary. Or maybe she would have walked out before telling Tracy about us.

The idea that she might take Kia away was worse than if the baby she was carrying wasn't mine. I slumped against the chair to slow my breathing. I'd been nursing my anger for so long it was like an appendage. Even if I cut it off, I was sure phantom pains would riddle me.

A nurse opened the door, looked at her file and said, "Sasha Samuels."

Sasha was out of her seat before me, following the nurse through the opened door without checking to see if I was behind her. She was on autopilot. I didn't even need to be there, she would have stuck the results to my forehead when she got them.

The nurse inquired about her health and took her weight and blood pressure. "The doctor should be right in. Strip from the waist down and use this to cover up." She handed Sasha a stiff paper wrap. "You can have a seat right there." She said to me and pointed to a chair in the corner.

Maybe I was being punished, relegated to a position on the sidelines. We waited in silence. Sasha still refused to talk to me or look at me. But I couldn't explain why I needed to know, again. I was out of words.

The doctor came into the room. "Good morning," his tone was pleasant. If he had any indication what we were going through he never let on.

He performed what I guess was a customary examination, then applied gentle pressure to her stomach.

"Doctor, I'd like to have a paternity test done," she said without preamble. The doctor glanced over at me, looking over his glasses.

"After the baby is born?" His attention was back on the file.

"No, now. I've done some research on the Internet. I know it's possible and I don't want to wait until later. We really need to know and seven months is too long to worry."

He pushed his stool away from the examination table. After looking from me, then back to Sasha, he rubbed his hands together. "I see. Do you think this is something that needs to happen right now? My advice would be to wait." His voice was unsteady. He looked like he wanted to say more.

"I don't want to wait." Sasha had removed her feet from the stirrups and tightened the gown around her nakedness.

"You're aware there are risks?" He spoke slowly.

Sasha took a deep breath and glanced in my direction. "I am. But in this situation we don't have much choice."

"What are the risks?" I found my voice and leaned forward, pushing my way into the conversation.

"Well there are two types, Amniocentesis and Chorionic Villus Sampling." He focused his attention on me, as if I was the easiest to reason with. "Both pose a slight risk of miscarriage and at its extreme, can cause some birth defects. I usually only request these tests if I think there is a problem with the pregnancy, not just to determine parentage."

"I don't care. I can't live like this anymore. The way I'm feeling I just might lose the baby anyway. At least this way the doubt is erased and we can go our separate ways and live our lives."

"Wait a minute," I said.

"I hope you don't mind me asking, but did

254

something happen? Were you assaulted?" the doctor asked.

I looked at Sasha. "Why would you put the baby at risk this way?"

She burst into sobs. "I…I…you…" She pressed the tip of the gown to her face and released a big sob.

"I had no idea this was dangerous. We can't do this." There was panic in my voice, but I tried to be calm. Someone had to be reasonable, and it wasn't going to be Sasha. "Can you please give us a minute, doctor?" I asked, almost shoving him aside as I came to stand next to her.

When we were alone, I tried to hold her, but she pushed me away. "This is what you want, isn't it? It's the only thing that matters to you?"

"That's not true. I never wanted you to jeopardize your health or the baby's. I was willing to wait." I reached for her again and she allowed me to hold her.

"What will you do Walter? Sneak the baby off one day while I'm out and have a paternity test done behind my back. I guess that's more your style, isn't it?"

I froze. I could feel the blood draining from my face, pooling in my ankles. Dreading my behavior, I never wanted anyone to know about the test. "How did you know?"

"I found the paper, shoved in your drawer when I was putting your laundry away."

Having a discussion about our lives in a sterile

doctor's office was inappropriate, but this was the opportunity I was given and the one I had to use. Maybe it was all my bolstering and ill temper, but Sasha looked too fragile. If the test she thought she needed to exonerate her reputation didn't make her miscarry, then the pressure I was pushing on her certainly would.

Her tears had slowed and instead of the loud gasping sounds, now she simpered like an unhappy child.

"How long have you known about the paternity test?"

"For over a week." With her hands clasped in her lap, she fiddled with her engagement ring.

"Why didn't you say anything?"

"I wasn't surprised. You're not as complicated as you may think. The way you're acting now...as if I'm trying to trap you...or that I'm lying to you...it doesn't matter now. Nothing matters right now, but this. Once you've got the proof you need, we can discuss how we're going to handle Kia."

"I can't let you do this. This test is too dangerous. What is the rush? I'm willing to wait."

"I'm not. Not for seven months. I'm not stoic like Tracy. I won't play the role of the long-suffering girlfriend waiting around until you think I'm worth fighting for. The only person you really care about is yourself. If something doesn't meet your timeline, or if something doesn't please you, you're ready to drop it and move to a pasture that meets your needs. Well, that might be fine for you. And it might make you happy for a while, but that's not the life I want. You left Tracy's house and moved in with me, but you were never really with me. You were only biding your time until something new and shiny came along to rescue you from the mundane."

I pulled the chair closer and sat in it. With my head in my hands and my eyes closed, I tried to think through this mess. I had to get comfortable with the bed I'd made for myself and stop going backwards.

I couldn't get Tracy back.

I couldn't erase the damage I'd caused with Sasha.

And I couldn't be happy without Kia in my life.

Too many lives were entangled in it for me to walk away from. In the end, I wanted Kia to look at me and be proud.

I had to find a way to examine my *own* reflection and be happy.

If Sasha was so compelled to put her baby on the line to prove a point, what did it say about her? She had come to the place where she couldn't be pushed any further. Taking her stand. It was time for me to do the same thing.

"Please don't do this. You've made your point," I said.

"So what will you do?"

"Whatever I do, it's my issue. The problem is in

my head." I touched her stomach for the first time since she told me she was pregnant. "It's my baby and I don't want anyone to poke at him." I handed her the clothes she'd worn into the office. "Let's go home. We can figure this out."

Chapter Twenty-Nine - Tracy

Marco gripped my hand. I knew he wouldn't let it go and that is the only thing that kept me upright in the chair while we waited for the doctor to enter the room. From the time we got in the car to make the drive to the appointment, I repeated the same mantra in my head. *It's going to be all right. It's going to be all right.*

"Are you okay?" Marco squeezed my hand. The intensity in his eyes was so fierce I could almost believe that he could take on cancer and win.

"I'm fine." I lied, but it was time to be the big girl. If this was going to happen to me, I had to be strong for Marco. For Crystal. For my mother.

The door opened. "Sorry to keep you waiting." Dr. Jefferies settled behind the desk. Her white lab coat still held its crisp creases even though she had to be nearing the end of her workday.

"This is my husband, Marco Ferrara."

"Nice to meet you, Marco." She reached across the large desk and shook his hand, then turned to me. "I know you must be anxious, but I wanted you to come in so we could chat." She ruffled through papers on the center of her desk, using her index finger to scan the page.

I refused to take a breath.

"The mass in your breast was benign—"

"Oh my God, did you say benign. That means I don't have cancer, right?" I jumped out of the chair, dragging Marco with me. He embraced me in a hug that gave me my future back. "Oh my God. Oh my God." I was shaking. "I…I…when you called, I thought it was to tell me the lump was cancerous."

The doctor placed her hand on her chest. The color drained from her face. "I'm so sorry. I should have thought about that, or I should have told the assistant to let me talk to you directly."

"Is there something more you wanted to say doctor?" Marco draped his arm around my shoulders holding me in place.

"Well, Tracy, you mentioned wanting to start a family. We never finished that conversation after we found the lump, so I wanted to give you the results of the biopsy and also talk to you about getting pregnant."

My audible exhale stopped her. My heart raced like a wild pony. The thought of having a baby had evaporated with the worry that had taken over my life.

"Is there a problem?" I asked, starting the health care turmoil again.

"There are some things you need to be aware of. Women of a certain age…" She was trying to be delicate. "Need to be aware of some concerns."

"Wait a minute, before we talk about having babies, I need to talk about my breasts. What do I need to do, going forward, about them?"

She adjusted her position in the chair. "Some people have dense breast, it's not good or bad, it just is. For a while, we'll check your breasts every six months, and make sure you get your mammograms on schedule." Her explanation was simple. After weeks of trying to outrun the threat of death, the fog lifted and my life could return to normal.

I faced Marco, the lines around his mouth had disappeared and even if he'd never admit it to me, I could see the relief in his eyes.

Marco stood up. "Dr. Jefferies, I don't mean to be rude, but I don't want to talk about babies right now. I want to take my wife home and digest the news that she's healthy and doesn't have cancer. Having a baby isn't as important as having her back. We'll come back, together," he paused and looked down at me. "We'll let you give us that whole speech about middle aged folks procreating when we're ready, because right now neither one of us will hear a word you're saying."

I stood too. "He's right. I'm not living in fear anymore. I'm just living with all the hurt and trouble that comes with life, but I'm not going to sit around and hold my breath and wait on it. It's going to have to catch me."

The doctor nodded. "I understand. Call me if we need to have that conversation."

Marco and I darted out of her office. In minutes

we were going down in the elevator to the car. Every time we looked at each other, one of us managed to giggle.

"How should we spend the rest of our day?" he asked me when we exited the parking lot.

"Not cooped up in an office or looking at computer screens. We need to take a ride, run on a beach, and make love like it's our first time."

"I know just the place." He took the exit for Route One.

"Where are we going?"

"To *A Corner of Heaven.* The weather is just right for a walk on the beach." He glanced at me for a moment before returning his gaze to the road.

"The Outer Banks?" I couldn't have heard him correctly. "Marco, that's over a six hour drive."

"And we've got all the time in the world."

Chapter Thirty - Crystal

Mom was meeting me at the train station in Wilmington. Being with her seemed the best place to start putting my life back together. The red brick train station, even though it looked a little run down, lifted my spirits. There was comfort in the familiar.

I caught the elevator from the platform, half expecting, half hoping to see my mother waiting for me at the bottom of the stairs.

The more distance I put between New York and me, the more distance I put between Max and me. But it didn't matter, he'd walked out of the apartment and I hadn't seen him since. Why did he think he could keep disappearing? What was I supposed to do?

"Crystal." My mother waved. "Over here."

I reached her and wrapped my arms around her. She returned the hug. Her warmth welcomed me home like nothing else could.

"You look good," I said when I released her. "Compared to the last time I saw you…"

"Oh, if only you knew how great I feel now. I probably shouldn't have told you about the test. I should have waited until it was all over. I never told your grandmother. Can you imagine what she would have done?" We walked outside of the station along with the other commuters. The sun was already setting behind the building. "She probably would have come to stay with me and made me hot tea every

263

day."

"Is that what you have planned for me? I could use some tea. Lots of it."

She squeezed my shoulders, the same way she used to when I came home with sad stories. "I'll do whatever you need. Starting tonight." Once we were in the car, she said, "Do you want to talk about what happened between you and Max?"

I put on my seatbelt and stared out the window so she couldn't see my face. "No. It wouldn't make you very proud of me."

"You could never do anything that would make me abandon you. Relationships are hard. No one knows that better than me."

"I'll talk about it, just not right now. It's long, drawn out, and ugly," I said.

"What do you want, Crystal, from your life?"

"No one has asked me that since I was a little girl? Why doesn't anyone ask grownups that question more often?"

"I guess everyone figures once you get grown, you can get whatever you want."

"Well, either I'm not grown or I missing a vital adult gene, because I've never been more confused than I am right now."

We drove the short distance home without answers to my questions. She helped me unload my bags from the car and to get settled. Boxes lined one wall of the bedroom where I was going to be sleeping until I found my own place.

"I see you guys are moving soon." I eyed all the packing material and felt a little stranded. My mother continued to move away from everything I knew, my memories good and bad, and into a life I knew nothing about. We couldn't sit down and laugh about anything more recent than a few months. Part of it was my fault. I'd been the one to cut her off so I could nurture my hostility uninterrupted.

"Next week." She walked up beside me. "There's a room for you at the new house. I made sure of it."

I turned to her with the sting of tears in my eyes. She always had that uncanny way of knowing what I was thinking. I wondered when my instincts would become fine-tuned enough to pick up on the things that people didn't always say. All I could do was nod and hold on to her.

"Oh, Mom, I made such a mess of everything." I couldn't hold back the tears any longer. Memories of the last few months surged back like a giant wave. She led me to the bed and we sat.

I buried my head in her shoulder and cried. "I can't see any way for my life to turn around and be happy again."

She rocked me back and forth. "It's going to be okay, Crystal. It really is, darling. I know some pain feels like it's cutting so deep you'll split in two, but time is the balm that will put you back together. You've just got to allow the process to work. Open up

265

and let it work."

"I cheated on Max." There I'd said it. I thought telling her would make her revolt against me, instead she tightened her arms. Not asking any questions. "I feel so dirty. I don't feel like I should ever be forgiven, and if Max has anything to say about it, I won't."

She remained quiet, but continued to rock me. I think the motion was soothing her, too.

"I can't even tell you why I did it. I didn't love Dexter. Not the way I loved Max. But he was there. He was nice to me, interested in me. Whenever we were together, I could forget all the bad stuff, the stuff that made me sad. But I never loved him. I loved the idea of him. Does that make any sense?"

"No one has to validate what you feel. Simply because you felt it, that's validation enough." The compassion in her voice was enough to start a new stream of tears.

"I didn't mean to hurt Max…well, yes I did, but I thought he was having an affair. He left me," I said between crying jags.

"Remember when you were in high school and you thought that cheerleader had started a rumor about you?" She pulled away from me and looked into my eyes.

I nodded.

"And so you scrawled on the girl's restroom wall, *Jennie Mason is a whore.*"

I flinched as the memory of both my parents sitting with me in the principal's office while I tried to explain that I had been the one wronged. That Jennie had started the whole series of events. But my Calculus teacher had caught me in the act, so I was the one who had to spend a week in detention.

"I remember," I whispered.

"Do you remember what I said to you back then?"

I nodded again. My words seemed to get lost somewhere between my head and my mouth.

"*While seeking revenge, dig two graves - one for yourself.* My mother found that quote when I was a little girl. Whenever I was upset with someone and wanted to get back at them, she'd remind me of it."

"I guess you should have said it to me more than once. Obviously, it didn't stick after one time," I said.

"I know you didn't approve of the way I handled your father when all that…that stuff came out, but I couldn't let that drag me down to a level that would have destroyed me. I was hurt for a long time, but I knew striking out at Walter or Sasha wasn't going to make me feel better in the end."

"I've been judging you for so long, I feel like I was looking through dark glasses for years. I thought you were weak and pathetic for not lashing out. But at least you didn't destroy everything in your way. Your actions were ladylike and effective. I'm sorry for the way I treated you," I said.

"Don't be. I understand it was difficult for you

and you were handling it the best way you knew how. Give yourself some time."

I soaked up her words, not really believing them. There were so many things I could have done different. Better. She said I needed time. It had been weeks and I still felt raw and exposed.

"I don't think he'll ever forgive me."

"He might not. But it won't kill you. You'll be okay. Trust me. Have you heard from him?"

"Not in weeks. He won't take my calls."

There was a soft knock on the door. "Hey, can I come in?" Marco asked.

My mother looked at me and I nodded my approval. He came in and my mother released me to stand and give him a kiss. I saw something between them that I never saw with my father. The way they looked at each other, like it was the first time. The way Marco slipped one arm around her waist, pulling her close, even for the quick kiss. I was ashamed for wanting to deny my mother this happiness. What kind of child would?

"Buonasera, Crystal?"

"Ciao," I said.

"I'm sorry to hear about you and Max. You know you're welcome here for as long as you like." He bent down and kissed my forehead.

I couldn't respond. The gesture was probably nicer than I deserved.

"Let's give her a few minutes to get settled."

Mom looked at me.

"Yes, get settled and prepare for an authentic Italian meal of spaghetti. It should be ready in about thirty minutes. I've been simmering the sauce all day." Marco's good nature spread through the room like a soothing presence. I couldn't help but smile.

I drove up to Sasha's house and parked Mom's car on the street. This was only my second visit to this house. The place my father called home. I headed up the driveway and onto the concrete walk leading to the front entry.

He opened the door before I reached it.

"Is everything okay?" His eyes were wide and his feet were bare.

"Yes, Dad, I'm fine." I tried to reassure him. He held me at arm's length and looked me over like he expected to see visible injuries.

"I wasn't expecting a call from you. I guess it was just a surprise to hear your voice…you never call me." He stepped aside and let me enter the house in front of him.

In the den that was scattered with Kia's toys, he pointed to the sofa and sat beside me.

"Where are Sasha and Kia?" I glanced around. I needed to talk to my Dad. I wanted privacy.

"They're upstairs. I told Sasha you were coming

by and we needed to talk, alone."

"It's not that I'm trying to exclude—"

He brushed the comment aside. "She understands. It's no problem. Is it Max?" He still sounded anxious.

"We're separated, Dad. We'll probably file for divorce soon," I said.

"Oh, Crystal, I'm so sorry. Is this something you wanted?" He grabbed my hands and squeezed them.

"Let me say, it's because of me, but it's not something I want. I've told Mom all about it and I wanted to share it with you. I cheated on him."

His nose scrunched with hurt. I could tell he was bewildered. Who would have guessed that I would have been so much like him? He fell back against the sofa and rubbed his hands down his face.

"I won't go into detail. I'm sure you don't want to hear all that, but…but I don't think he'll be able to forgive. So it's time to move on."

He looked like he was weighing my response. After several seconds he said, "Okay. But how are you doing? Did you come all the way here just to tell me that? How can I help you, baby." He straightened up, gaining his composure. I recognized his look, he was ready to be my father and fix my mess.

"I don't need anything. I understand my behavior and I needed to apologize to you. I've treated you horribly, even worse than I did Mom and I'm sorry. I was so angry, I didn't even try to understand how the two of you were feeling."

"Well, part of that was our fault," he paused. "We were so messed up we catered to your every desire. It was our way of trying to look normal, to be normal. I don't think I ever said the word no to you."

"I don't think you did. But I'm not looking for excuses."

He pulled me into his arms, hugging me tight. "You know, when I was a little girl I knew about everything going on between you and mom." My voice was low, as if I was telling a secret. "I used to get out of bed and listen to you two fighting. I never understood why mom put up with it."

"I never knew that," he said.

"Yeah, I was a sneaky little kid. Always looking and listening for stuff I would have been better off not knowing about."

We rested on the sofa, facing the television that he must have muted when he heard me pull up.

"Your mother was a saint. I often wondered why she didn't leave me sooner. I'm sure you were the only thing holding us together."

"How long are you going to be in Delaware? Are you heading back tonight?"

"I'm here indefinitely." My gaze was focused on my wedding band and engagement ring. I hadn't removed either one yet. Maybe tonight.

"Where are you staying?"

"I'm with Mom and Marco. For now, anyway. Soon I'll make a decision and I promise to let you know."

He nodded and we were quiet for a moment.

"If you think you want to save your marriage, then don't wait. Do it now. Tell him you love him. If you wait too long, you might regret it," he said.

"You're thinking about Mom aren't you?"

"I finally know it's over and I've accepted it. But there was a window of time when I could have changed everything, won her back. At least I want to believe there was. So if there is a window of opportunity for you, grab it and make it work." His voice was so intense.

I patted his hand. "Okay." I wanted to appease him.

"Have you had dinner? I'm sure we have some leftovers." He started to push off the sofa.

"No, no. Marco cooked a wonderful dinner. I'm full," I said.

He looked at me for a long time. I could tell he wanted to say something more.

"Your mother, she's happy?" He didn't look at me.

I squeezed his hand. "She looks very happy. Marco is a good man and it's obvious they are in love with each other."

His eyes clouded over and he simply nodded his head.

Chapter Thirty-One - Walter

Across the breakfast table Kia made a mess with her Cheerios, smashing them into the tray on her high chair, but she looked happy and well adjusted. The last few months had been the most harmonious since the day she was born. It took me turning my life upside down to realize I was the one causing the discord residing in the house with us.

"Down, Daddy. Down." She beckoned to me with her baby spoon.

"Are you done eating?"

She bobbed her head and raised her arms, dropping more cereal on the floor. That simple gesture always melted my heart because it let me know she still needed me. I released the constraints and pulled the tray away. I lifted her out and she scurried away.

"Kia, come back in here. I want to be able to see you." I said, knowing that if she got distracted she'd wander well beyond the kitchen.

She strolled back in the room, dragging a stuffed rabbit behind her. I couldn't help but smile at her innocent round face.

Sasha probably wasn't aware that she was humming. But from the stove, the quiet melody could only come from her if she was happy. And I think she was. Last night she came to me willingly, which she hadn't done in months.

She sat back down at the table and wiped up the mush that Kia seemed so happy to produce. "I think we should tell her now." She rubbed her belly, which could no longer be ignored.

"She might not understand, but I agree. We should." My tone was soft, no curt replies or raised voices. I'd vowed never to talk to her like that again. I had vowed so many things to calm her down and make her feel comfortable. I had to show her by my actions. And now I was seeing the results. She was no longer contemplating walking out on me.

I picked up Kia and positioned her on my knee. She squirmed to get down. "We have something to tell you," I said.

Kia looked at her mother with wide eyes.

Sasha leaned close to Kia. Their noses almost touching. "Would you like to have a brother?"

Kia seemed to give the idea serious thought. Her head turning from Sasha back to me. "No," she shouted and tried to squirm out of my grip.

"You're going to have a brother in about three months," Sasha lifted her top, exposing her taut belly.

Kia pointed at the roundness.

"He's in here right now and he'll be here in a few months. The doctor says it's a boy. Aren't you excited?"

Kia shook her head, not nearly as excited by the news as we had been. She stiffened her little body until I released her.

"Well, we tried," I said, leaning forward and placing both my hands around Sasha's stomach. She was so excited when she found out it was going to be a boy. Finally she was able to give me something no one else had. The pride that showed on her face helped absolve me of some of my guilt.

A secret call to the doctor and he reminded me I was supposed to use protection for at least a month following the vasectomy. How I could have forgotten such a vital piece of the whole process still made my stomach churn, but the idea of having a son had grown on me, softening the blow from my own stupidity.

I pulled Sasha into my lap. She leaned her back against me and allowed me to continue to rub her stomach. I made a lot of promises to get us to this state. The woman that I had to win back turned out to be Sasha, and not Tracy after all. And the only way I could do it was to open myself up to whatever might happen. Even if she decided to stomp on my heart, I had no choice. Maybe someday I'd sneak off, without Sasha knowing, and have a paternity test done. But regardless of the results, the baby would always be mine and I'd never share the results with anyone.

I kissed her neck. "I've made the appointment for next week." I whispered in her ear before placing my tongue in it.

"I haven't agreed yet," she laughed. "You had plenty of opportunities to marry me, now I'm not so

275

sure I want to marry an old man." Her cracks about my age no longer stung. I knew she was joking.

"Yeah, but before you were trying to marry me. This time I'm trying to marry you. And you know I always get what I want."

"And now you're sure you want me?" She turned slightly and caressed my face between her palms.

She was right to ask me. I'd been the one dancing around the issue for so long. Something was different, but I couldn't articulate what. That feeling of needing to run had vanished some time ago, one day it was there and the next day I didn't notice it, much like taking the training wheels off and peddling into a new life. The sereneness around me wasn't as foreign as I'd imagined.

"I'm sure, next week at the courthouse in Elkton. Crystal and Kia will be there as our witnesses. Crystal has even agreed to watch Kia while I sweep you away for two glorious nights. Once you have the baby, we'll do a real honeymoon."

She turned completely around and straddled my lap. "I love you, so much."

"I love you, too. I don't know why it took me so long to figure it out."

I may not have the life I'd envisioned, but at least I was learning to love the life I had.

Chapter Thirty-Two - Crystal

Kia and I stood behind Dad and Sasha in the middle of the small courtroom. This had to be the happiest section in the whole building. As soon as they were married, there were several other couples waiting to take their place in front of the judge.

Maybe Sasha was good for Dad. He couldn't keep his hands off of his soon-to-be-wife and she appeared to enjoy every touch. The simple dress and flat shoes Sasha wore was a change, too. Something about being pregnant made Sasha more likable. I'd never call her mom, but I'd stopped calling her all the other names I'd reserved for her.

"I now pronounce you husband and wife. You may kiss your bride," the judge said.

Dad pulled her forward. He must have forgotten he was standing in front of a crowded room, because I would have sworn his tongue reached the back of Sasha's throat. If he didn't feel that way for Mom anymore, then he was right to go and find happiness.

I couldn't help but be sad when I should have been happy. I still called, and occasionally Max picked up the phone, but the conversation was always filled with caution. His monotone responses let me know that he stood on one side of the chasm and I was still on the other. The time that Mom promised was going to heal me hadn't erased all the pain yet. But I was doing better. The anger that used to simmer in my stomach like a witch's brew was gone now. With nobody to focus my outrage on, I realized I was the only one living in the past. Mom and Marco and Dad and Sasha, and even Max had all moved on. It was time for me to do the same.

"Mommy," Kia yelled, pulling away from me and grabbing her mother's leg as soon as the simple ceremony was done.

"Pumpkin, your mom and dad are married now. So when your brother comes, we'll be just like that family in your bedtime story book." Sasha said when she picked Kia up.

"Come to me, you're too heavy for Mommy." Walter held out his arms and Kia jumped into them.

"I'm glad you came to support us, Crystal," Sasha reached her hand out to me. "As you can see, we didn't have anyone else here."

"Dad, why didn't you invite grandma and your brothers?"

He shook his head and placed his hand on Sasha's belly. He might have been able to move forward with Sasha, but with his mother, he was still stuck in his childhood.

"We didn't want to make a big deal of it. We almost didn't make it to this point, so this is special and we wanted to keep it very low key," Sasha spoke up.

"Let's go to lunch. We have a small celebration planned at Banks Brunch."

I followed Dad and his new wife out of the restaurant. With Dad holding Kia in one arm and holding hands with Sasha, they looked like the perfect couple who'd never seen a day of turmoil.

If only Max could have been there to witness the day, then maybe he could believe in miracles. I pushed those thoughts away. Living in the past didn't serve me well. The last time I gave into them I was depressed much too long. The last few months had been relatively happy and I wanted to keep it that way.

#####

I came through the foyer of the new bungalow to find Mom seated on the floor with an array of photo albums scattered in front of her.

"Are you still unpacking?" I asked before flopping down on the sofa in front of her.

"Yes and it's tedious. I think it's going to take more than a year to sort out what we want and what we need to get rid of. How was the wedding?" I was proud of her tone, there was nothing hiding behind her question. My parents had turned into civilized people.

"I think he's really happy. Maybe because Sasha is having a boy this time, but he's changed. In a good way."

"That's good to hear. Now you have two normal

parents," she said. "So help me sort through this stuff. See if there are any pictures you'd like to have." She pushed a box of photos towards me.

I kicked off my heels. "Do I have to? Can't you just keep my stuff here? I promise to get it one day. I looked at a two bedroom unit the other day at the River Front." I settled on the floor beside her. "I've been meaning to tell you I got a raise."

She squealed. "That's wonderful, Crystal. Why are you just now telling me?"

"Well, when I came home last night, you and Marco were busy."

She blushed and dropped her head. "I see. We were christening the house," she murmured.

I reached over and rubbed her shoulder. "I'm just happy you're so happy. If you and Dad can find happiness, than maybe I can, too. Because the two of you were the most miserable people I knew."

She gave me a playful swat. "Even worse than you and Max?"

"Yes, because you two were at it longer. Max and I put our relationship out of its misery in less than two years." There was only a little sadness in my voice.

"You were right, you know," I said.

"About what?"

"About time healing me. I don't feel as raw anymore. Some days I almost feel like a normal person," I said.

"I can tell. At least now you're smiling more. I

think I heard you laughing while you were talking to your friend the other day."

The doorbell rang and saved me from the dismay creeping down my neck.

Marco came out of the kitchen. "Were you two expecting anyone?"

We said *no* in unison.

"I'd better get it then." He stepped over the mess and made his way to the foyer.

A moment later he returned. "Crystal."

I turned to see Max standing next to Marco. My body went rigid. All I could do was stare and try to figure out what he was doing in my mother's house.

Both Mom and Marco looked uncomfortable.

"I did it, Crystal. I gave him the address," my mother said. "He called my cell and begged me. Don't be mad honey, but I think you two need to talk." She unfolded her legs and stood. Marco slipped his hand around her waist and led her out of the room.

I struggled to my feet, my knees almost refused to cooperate. He advanced into the room and helped me up. Just the smell of his cologne took me back to happier times. I hadn't seen him since the day he walked out of the condo in New York for the second time. The tortured look was gone. To the outside world, we probably looked like two ordinary people. This had to be what my mother was talking about. The scars might not go away, but I was the only one who could see them. There was even a peacefulness that had settled over me.

"I'm surprised to see you." My voice trembled. I hoped he couldn't hear it. I wasn't ready for the conversation. As soon as I got up my nerve I had planned to call him and say the hardest thing I ever had to say.

"I miss you." He looked in my eyes and held my gaze. It was so intense I almost looked away, but something refused to release me. "The only thing I wanted to do was to forget about you...but it didn't work."

My heart constricted. I braced for him to finish.

"But I can't." He took a deep breath. "Are you seeing someone?"

I shook my head. "No. I've been missing you. And I can't forgive myself. I was horrible—"

"I don't want to go backwards." He lifted my left hand from my side. "You're still wearing your rings?"

"Yeah. I wasn't ready to take them off." I fought the overwhelming urge to cry. I was terrified he was there to ask me for a divorce.

"Your mom said you were working."

I stepped back to the sofa and flopped down. "I am." I wanted to say more, but I still couldn't believe he was standing in my mother's living room. I gestured for him to sit beside me. "I'm really sorry about—"

He put up his hand to stop me. "I'm hoping there

is still a future for the two of us."

My body relaxed, allowing me to feel the warmth of his words. "I can't come back to New York. I know you didn't ask me to, but I need to be honest with you."

"Honesty is a good start. And I promise to always put you first. Always."

I couldn't fight back the tears any longer.

One Year Later – Crystal

I stared at my reflection in the full-length mirror, quite surprised at the sense of calm surrounding me. A year ago, I wasn't certain about anything, least of all me and Max. But today, everything was perfect. The weather was warm with just enough of a breeze to keep the humidity from being oppressive. I was having a good hair day, my curls had plenty of bounce and everybody I loved was in the house.

Max stepped out of the closet. In his tuxedo he was even more handsome than usual and once again my heart seemed to tumble in my chest.

"Tell me again we're doing the right thing," I said.

He crossed the room and placed his hands on my shoulders. "I have no doubt, we're doing the right thing."

"Yes, but the last time—"

He put his index finger against my lips. "Remember we promised not to look back, only forward." He held my gaze.

"And you've forgiven me?" I still asked that question almost monthly. My therapist said I needed to forgive myself.

"I have. And have you forgiven me?" he asked.

"I have."

He wrapped his arms around me and gave me a deep kiss. All at once, I felt warm and safe. Somehow we managed to save our marriage. It was hard and there were so many times when I thought one of us would think it wasn't worth the effort.

There was a soft knock on the door and my mother entered the master bedroom without waiting for me to respond.

"I'm sorry, Max. I thought you were in the garden already," she said before entering.

"I'm on my way now." He gave me a long look before exiting.

"Oh my, Crystal." My mother placed her hand at her throat. "You look amazing. I know it's a simple dress, but it's perfect for the occasion."

She came to stand in front of me.

"Thank you, Mom." I pecked her cheek. "You don't think it's silly for us to have this little ceremony? Most people wait until they've been married a few years before they renew their vows or have a grand gesture. We've been married for less than three years."

"Honey, not at all. You and Max have worked hard to save your marriage. After all the therapy sessions, the date nights, the homework, I think it's an excellent way to recommit to each other." Her eyes were glassy, she was about to cry.

"Please don't start crying or I'll start too." I ran my hand over the cream-colored midi dress. The gold beading around the waist gave the dress its only touch of flair.

I turned back to the mirror and applied my lip

gloss. I'm sure Max and I would always have the scars from the way we had treated each other, but maybe they would be the glue that held us together, forever. We were moving ahead, leaving all the ugly stuff behind us.

"Did you guys make a decision about going away- a honeymoon?"

"We decided to wait a while. Maybe for Christmas we'll steal away for a few days. Max is happy running his own practice. I'm enjoying my new assignment." I shrugged my shoulders. "We're in a good place. We're talking about starting our family." I glanced over at my mother to see her dab a tissue to her eyes.

"Don't give me that look. I'm just so happy. One day I'm going to be a grandmother."

"Yes, one day, but give us a few months." I pecked her cheek, careful not to smear my lip gloss. "We're taking everything much slower this time."

"Is he happy about being back in Delaware?" she asked.

I turned to her. "He is. We both are. His practice probably won't afford us an apartment on 5th Avenue in New York, but we'll probably be able to buy a nice house in Greenville," I said.

"Next to the Bidens'?" I could tell she was amused by her comment because her eyes twinkled with mischief.

"Maybe." I reached for her hand and pulled her

up. "Now we better get downstairs. I don't want to keep everyone waiting."

I followed her out of the bedroom. At the top of stairs, I touched her shoulder to get her attention. "Thanks, Mom. For everything," I whispered.

"For what, honey?"

"You know." I paused to push back the tears threatening to ruin my make-up. "For you and dad putting your stuff aside so that I could have my whole family here today."

"What happened between your father and me is history. We both only wanted the best for you." She placed her palm on my cheek and used her thumb to brush away a tear. "You deserve to be happy."

"Crystal, come on down. I think if Max has to wait another minute he's going to burst." My father called from the foot of the stairs. He held his son in his arms. The baby squirmed to break free.

"Who names a little boy, Sebastian," Mom whispered.

"It was Sasha's idea. I think he's named after her." I tried to whisper, too.

"Figures," she said before heading down the stairs.

"I heard that." He released the toddler but continued to hold her hand. "The name was my idea. I sure didn't want to saddle him with a moniker like Walter."

"It's a fine name, I was only joking. Now let's get

outside."

We followed Mom into the small garden that Max and I had spent a fortune to get ready for the day. Planters of roses lined the perimeter and provided the touch of festivity we needed. Max stood under the trellis he and Marco had assembled the day before and, for a moment, I almost swooned. Without the formality of being escorted to Max, I had to take a deep breath and gather myself.

The ceremony wasn't a legal or religious requirement so our therapist conducted our vow renewal. He stood under the trellis in front of Max.

"We are gathered here today to support Maxwell and Crystal as they recommit to each other. The past is behind them. The only thing that matters for them is the future and the vows they've written will affirm that. Crystal has agreed to go first."

I turned to face Max and held his hands. "My dearest Max, from this day forward, I vow to love you, trust you, and to be faithful to you. I vow to communicate my feelings and never to go to bed angry. You're the man I want to share my life with and I plan to spend the rest of my life showing you." I slipped his original wedding band on his ring finger.

He cleared his throat. His eyes were as glassy as Mom's had been earlier. "Crystal, my love, from this day forward, I will put you in the center of my life. Nothing I do will come before you. Every day I vow not only to tell you I love you, but to show you just how much." He stared into my eyes as he slipped my wedding rings on my finger.

The same wave of emotions from earlier rose in my stomach again, making my knees almost buckle.

Our therapist stepped forward. "Before the witnesses you've selected today, Maxwell and Crystal, you start your new life. You may kiss your bride."

Before Max could bend down to me, I pulled him forward, cupped my hands around his neck and kissed him like I'd done the night before, when we were alone.

"I meant every word," he said in my ear.

"So did I."

JOIN THE JACKI KELLY NEWSLETTER!

At

JACKIKELLY.COM

So you can stay tuned to new releases, appearances, events and prizes. She's away giving away something.

<u>ABOUT THE AUTHOR</u>

Jacki Kelly has written dozens of short stories and several books. She lives in the North East with her husband and one loveable dog. She loves hearing from her readers so please contact her.

Connect with her online:
http://www.jackikelly.com
Twitter - @jackikellybooks
http://facebook.com/jackikellyauthor

If you enjoyed reading Going Backwards, please tell everyone you know. Please post a review for other readers on Amazon, Barnes and Noble, Goodreads or other forums.

Made in United States
North Haven, CT
29 July 2024

55544760R10178